The Safe House

The Safe House

A World War II Story

Edward Lynd Kendall

Library of Congress Control Number:		2010902105
ISBN:	Hardcover	978-1-4500-4481-3
	Softcover	978-1-4500-4480-6
	Ebook	978-1-4500-4482-0

This book was printed in the United States of America.

To order additional copies of this book, contact:
Xlibris Corporation
1-888-795-4274
www.Xlibris.com
Orders@Xlibris.com
76887

Dedication

This work is dedicated to the men and women of the Eighth Air Force, who, in the face of almost insurmountable odds, conducted bombing raids deep into the heart of Germany, paving the way for final victory over the evil Nazis Empire, and saving the world for democracy. I also wish to celebrate the courageous work of the Dutch Underground in saving so many Allied airmen forced to bail out over Holland.

ACKNOWLEDGMENTS

I wish to express my appreciation for the endless hours my wife, Mary Ann, has spent reading and rereading the manuscript. She probably didn't expect all of this when we first met in a Shakespeare class at the University of Michigan many years ago.

Many friends have assisted in reading and editing the manuscript: Gloria and Stewart Mansfield, Sandy Nicholson, Christina Gillerain and John Engle. I am also indebted to all the members of the Batavia Library Writers Group for helping me hone my skills as a writer.

Finally, I would like to thank my golfing friend, Mel Simmons, who piloted a B-24 on the most hazardous missions deep into Germany. His story of being protected by the Dutch underground provided the original ideas for this novel.

ABOUT THE BOOK

In May of 1944 the Allies were readying an invasion of the European Continent. At an English airbase an American crew was preparing their Liberator bomber, a B-24, heavily loaded with high octane gasoline and bombs, for takeoff into the murky overcast. Takeoff under these conditions was a perilous part of the mission. The odds were against them anyway with no fighter escort available all the way to their target, an aircraft plant, at Hamburg, Germany.

The experienced but young pilot, Captain James Scott, was close to relief back to the states with almost twenty five missions. The copilot, Bill Richter, was new to the crew, having just replaced an injured man. He had never flown a bomb run before.

This historical novel tells the parallel stories of these two young Americans, of very different character, forced to bail out over Holland after their engines fail. Their personal stories are set in the broader matrix of the momentous events of that last year of World War II in Europe. Other unforgettable characters include a courageous and patriotic Dutch housewife, a daring young resistance fighter, a Dutch businessman of questionable values and a little Jewish girl who escaped from the Nazis. It is a compelling and fast moving tale of heroism and cowardice, and a torrid romance with unforeseen consequences—of the potential for good and evil in the hearts of man.

ABOUT THE AUTHOR

Dr. Edward Kendall is an honors graduate in Liberal Arts from the University of Michigan. After military service in the Air Force during World War II he secured a Masters Degree and Ph.D. in clinical psychology from the University of Pittsburgh. He also completed an internship in clinical psychology with the Veterans Administration.

After graduation he joined an international management consulting firm in Chicago. For the next twelve years he traveled all over the country counseling with corporations in the areas of psychological assessment, organizational analysis, compensation and executive search. He advanced from staff psychologist, to manager and partner with this firm.

Subsequently, he formed a boutique consulting firm working in the above aspects and eventually broadened the practice to general management and leveraged buyouts. He also taught business managent courses to M.B.A candidates at De Paul and Northern Illinois universities.

During World War II he served as a Staff Sergeant in the Second Air Force as a mechanic, an inspector and a crew chief. His final assignment was as an air inspector certifying the airworthiness of aircraft at the Air Force College. Seeking to get into combat, he had volunteered for training as a flight engineer on long range bombers, the B-29's that had been rushed into production to provide the ability to bomb Japan from bases in India and return. When the war in Europe ended this program was discontinued.

Through his military service and study of psychology he is intimately familiar with the heavy bombers featured in this work and the stresses the aircrews were under in bombing Germany.

He has been married for sixty years and has a son and daughter and five grandchildren. He has traveled extensively throughout the country and Europe and is an avid golfer and skeet shooter.

Also By The Author

"The Case of Russian Roulette and Other Stories", a book of short stories.

"Too Much Testosterone", a short story.

"Requiem For Ed", a poem.

"Edward Lynd Kendall, A Personal History", an autobiography.

CHAPTER I

World War II

At the close of 1943 the world was at war. The major powers were engaged in the most horrendous conflict the world had ever known. After the early successes of Germany in occupying much of the continent, Hitler had anticipated a speedy invasion of England. Due to the heroic efforts of a relatively small number of English fighter pilots, with their Spitfire and Hurricane fighters, Germany was unable to attain air superiority over the island nation. The planned invasion of England proved impossible. After the United States came into the war, Hitler made the monumental mistake of invading Russia. Germany was soon on the defensive.

By the spring of 1944 the tide had turned. A massive buildup of men and equipment was underway in England prior to the invasion of the continent. The allies had encountered stiff resistance coming up through Italy, but in May, Rome was liberated. In the air war in the winter of 1943-1944 the heavy bombers were limited to short range targets due to heavy losses early on, because of the lack of fighter escort. But early in 1944, with the enhanced range of the American fighters, the Mustangs, and the increased numbers, allied bombers were unleashed to attack the enemy wherever it could be found. Heavy losses to the Luftwaffe resulted and they lost control of the air during the day. As a result long range missions into Germany became routine and inflicted heavy damage on the enemy.

Momentous events were to unfold during that last year of World War II.

Five A.M., May 28th, 1944, Eighth Air Force Base, Coldwater, England.

In the damp fog of an English morning, Captain Jim Scott was running the pre-flight check list on his B-24, as the copilot called out the items. Stressed and fatigued by the missions he'd flown, and a little hung over, he forced himself to carefully check every instrument. This mission promised to be especially hazardous, deep into the heart of Germany, to Hamburg with its heavy anti-aircraft batteries. He was close to the magic twenty five missions and return to the states but fearful this one might be jinxed.

Jim eased the bomb-laden aircraft into position behind a long line of B-24's, watching impatiently as they took off, one by one, into the murky overcast. With clearance from the tower, he pulled up to the front of the runway and gunned up the engines, running through the obligatory magneto checks. With no loss of power in any of the engines they were ready to go.

He extended the flaps, jammed the throttles to full power, and released the brakes. The battle-scarred '24 ponderously started its roll, lumbering down the runway, gradually picking up speed. With the bomb bays loaded and the tanks full, just getting aloft was a hazardous part of the mission. At the very end of the runway he pulled the yoke back with all his strength. Barely in time, they lifted off into the heavy overcast. He searched through the gloom for the squadron leader. Tight formations were essential to maximize fire power in case of attack. He breathed a sigh of relief when he spotted the leader through the clouds off his left wing, and pulled into position. As they headed out over the channel the sky cleared. The brilliant sun was a welcome sight. It would help in holding formation, but unfortunately it would also make it easier for Germany's prized fighter, the M.E. 109's, to spot them. The crew was heartened by the improved weather but worried about the added danger. When they crossed over Holland a flight of American P-47's joined them to provide fighter escort.

As the altimeter approached seven thousand feet, the captain came on the intercom, "Listen you guys, we're going up to twelve thousand. Put your oxygen masks on. Be sure they're working properly. If there are any problems report back to me."

After gaining the designated altitude, he spaced out listening to the droning of the engines. With the fighter escort and the clear weather it was the safest part of the trip. Jim daydreamed about his impending leave. Two more missions and he'd return to the states. He missed his mom and dad, and his girl friend, Suzy. No sex for months at a time had left him horny as a young bull. A few one night stands with English girls weren't like his one true love, Suzy.

Feeling relaxed, he turned to his copilot, "Bill, would you take over for a while? It's all quiet now. I could use a little break."

"Sure thing, Scotty, why don't you take a little nap."

"Let me know if anything out of the way happens." Jim closed his eyes and slumped back in the seat, determined to get some rest, but he knew he wouldn't be able to sleep.

Bill Richter was a new addition to the crew after the former copilot got shot up. He knew Jim was stressed out. Too many missions and too many friends killed had taken their toll. The odds were against you anyway. Only fifty percent of the air crews in any of the bomb groups made it out alive.

After an unexpected cat nap Jim woke with a start, as if his unconscious knew when there might be a problem. "How's number two doing, where we had that oil leak?"

"It's okay, Scotty. Pressure's good. Looks like they found the problem.

Captain, I often wondered. What'd you do in civilian life, if you don't mind me asking?"

"Seems like another life. I was a grad student at Harvard, studying to get a Ph.D. in history. Thought I'd teach in some university."

"Your family must be rich. How'd you afford it?"

"I got an athletic scholarship and worked as a graduate assistant."

"What'd you get it in?"

"The rings."

"I didn't know you were an athlete. The rings? That's a sport?"

"It certainly is. It's part of gymnastics. I worked really hard on it in high school. Thought, I'd have a chance. Not many go out for the rings."

"I can believe that. You know what, you are always thinking."

"I've got my Masters, how about you Bill?"

"I'm a pharmacist, like Dad. Has his own drugstore. I worked for him."

"Are you married?"

"Nah, just play the field."

"Sounds good to me."

In the bowels of the ship, the ball turret gunner, Sergeant Finkenstadt, settled back after the scary takeoff. He yelled at the tail gunner.

"Hey Herb, how're things back there?"

"Nothing but blue sky back here. Maybe this one'll be easy."

"Don't count on it. We sure could use some luck. That last mission when we got shot up was rotten. I think it's all preordained anyway."

"What do ya mean by that?"

"It's like God decides whether we'll make it or not. Is this our day or not? It just might be."

"Where'd you get that dumb idea?"

"In my philosophy class."

"You're getting me down with all this bull shit."

"I can't help it. It's what I think."

"It must be your religion. You're Jewish, aren't you?"

"I am, but what's that got to do with it? It's just something I thought up. Herb, don't you ever get scared?"

"Of course I do, just like everybody else. The only place they don't is in those stupid John Wayne movies."

"I used to like those, until I found out what war's really like."

"I can't argue with that. How about Clark Gable going on some real bomb runs? Now there's a real man."

For some strange reason, known only to the Germans, they didn't encounter any enemy fighters that day, even after the American fighters, the P-47's had to turn back. When they did have fighter escort all the way these missions deep into Germany were still hazardous. Sometimes, good fortune did seem to come their way. The flight that day deep into the heart of Germany was uneventful.

The banter of the two gunners was interrupted unceremoniously by the captain on the intercom, "This is Captain Scott. We're approaching Hamburg. The ack ack will be really heavy. Pat, get set for the bomb run, it won't be long now."

Pat Wilson, the bombardier, was already hunched over the Norden sight. "Don't worry, I'll be ready. It should be easy to pick it up today."

Bill chimed in, "It's great for us too, we're like sitting ducks. How can they miss?"

Turning the mike off, Jim flushed, "For Christ's sake man, knock it off! We can't afford talk like that."

"You can't deny it."

"Listen here, I don't want another word like that on this ship. Is that clear, sir? You're a commissioned officer, now act like one."

"Yes sir, sorry!" He couldn't believe the Captain had pulled rank on him.

Finkenstadt yelled again at Herb, "You know, all this bravery stuff the politicians talk about all the time, it's a bunch of crap. Do you really think every guy that gets injured is a hero?"

"Yeah, it's overrated. It's only a way to get us out here to get our butt shot off."

"We agree on that. I don't do this job because I'm so noble and brave. I just know it's my duty. I can't let you guys down. Besides, I'd like to save my own ass."

"I see what you mean. I never thought of it that way. I think you're right."

"I sure am."

Approaching the target area, Milton and Herb decided to tend to business and shut up.

CHAPTER II

"It's a bloody miracle"

Captain Scott came on again, "Listen you guys back there. Cut the bull. Pay attention. I heard some of that. There's heavy flak ahead."

Finkenstadt realized he had left the mike open while he was talking to Herb. The crew couldn't believe the scene in front of them. The sky was almost solid with black smoke. Jim had never seen anything like it, even with all his missions. But he knew he had to put it out of his mind and make the right decisions. Bill was wet with sweat under his flight suit. He'd heard all about these bomb runs, but never thought it'd be anything like this. He was scared shitless.

Horrified, they watched as the ship up ahead was hit and went into a tortuous death spin.

"Oh my God, did you see that? We're in for it!" Bill yelled.

Jim ignored him and calmly signaled the bombardier, "Give me some help. I can hardly make out the aircraft plant with all this smoke. We're about ready to make our run. When I'm over the target, you get a fix and take over."

"Roger, Captain, I can just make it out now. Stay on course and hold her steady.

"Bill, hit the switch, open the bomb bay doors!" Jim shouted.

They listened as the hydraulics slowly ground the doors open. They felt the drag on the ship. Now they were in the midst of the heaviest ack-ack yet. It was like an inferno, with explosions all around. Approaching their target, a German aircraft fighter plant, the ship shuddered from the concussion of a near miss. The air was rancid with the smell of gunpowder.

Jim, trying to conceal his concern, instructed the bombardier, "Can you see it? There it is. Take over."

"Roger."

Pat Wilson carefully steadied the ship, concentrating over the bomb sight. Just at the right moment he let them go. The crew watched in awe, as the large bombs drifted lazily down to the target. It had an air of unreality about it, as if they were momentarily frozen in time, and nothing could happen to them.

When they were all away, Pat yelled, "Pull her up quick, they're all off. Let's get the hell out of here."

Jim studied the explosions below, satisfied with the result, "Good job, Pat, we hit that son-of-a-bitch hard."

He pulled the lightened ship into a sharp climb, hoping to avoid the flak. Just as they started to gain altitude, it shuddered with a direct hit. They were engulfed in smoke and the pungent smell of explosives.

Finkenstadt shouted into the mike, "We're hit; the left outboard's on fire."

The calm voice of the captain came on, "What exactly do you see?"

Taking a deep breath, "We're hit, just like I said, sir. It's number one."

Jim looked back as the prop started to windmill and flames engulfed the stricken nacelle.

"Feather number one!" The ship started to rattle and shake, as if it might break up.

The copilot yelled, "Done."

They watched, as the prop ground mercifully to a stop and the shaking abated.

Jim said, "Now hit the fire extinguisher."

Bill hit the switch. They watched as the flames diminished and slowly subsided. All that was left were the remnants of black smoke. Jim increased the power on the remaining engines and banked to the right to get out of there. It was like a collective sigh of relief for the crew.

They were almost out of the thick of it, when, to their horror, they heard a horrific thump. The ship started shaking dangerously, worse than ever. Looking out to the left Jim saw that number two, left inboard, had also been hit. A worst case scenario! With two engines out, both on the same side, they slowly started into a spin, dangerously losing altitude.

"Hit the fire extinguisher on two. Feather it." He pulled back on the control column with all his might. "Help me pull her up; we've got to stop this spin."

Sweating bullets, Bill yelled, "Let's bail out!"

"We'd never have a chance, do what I said. Quick man!"

Working together, with all their strength, they were just able to pull out, but they were still losing altitude. They watched as the altimeter trended ominously down. Jim, in training, had rehearsed the procedure with two engines out, but never both on the same side.

Sucking it up, Bill said, "The flames are going out, maybe we've got a chance."

Now heading west, they were leaving the metropolitan area but still slowly losing altitude.

"Our only chance is to restart number two; it's the least damaged. I'll try to hold her steady and you give it a try." Jim said.

Bill cranked the starter on the injured engine time after time, but to no avail. When he was just about to give up, the engine caught, belching black smoke. He was amazed, the smoke slowly diminished and they regained partial power. "It's like a bloody miracle." He said. Now they were just able to maintain altitude. Straining with all his might, Jim could overcome the torque and keep her on the level.

He yelled back at the navigator, "Give me a heading to the channel. We've got to get our ass out of here. We'll aim for that base in central England where they have long runways.

After studying the maps, the navigator announced, "Our best heading will be due west to Holland. If worse comes to worse we'd have a decent chance if we have to bail out there. They have a strong underground."

"Good thinking. We might have to bail out yet, that engine's leaking oil."

"I'll give you an exact heading in a few minutes."

Jim increased the power on number two to counter the torque. It took all his strength to hold her steady. When his legs started to shake, he took turns with the copilot.

Going on the intercom, "All you guys check for damage in your area and report back. We're still losing altitude. Jettison everything movable to lighten the ship. That includes the guns and the ammo. We'll just have to take our chances with enemy aircraft."

The crew rushed to comply and reported back on damage. It was favorable except for Finkenstadt's warning.

"Captain, the nacelles on one and two are blackened and the skin on one is damaged."

"Any sign of structural damage?"

"Not that I can see."

"Good."

"You think we've got a chance, Captain?"

"I think we've got a good chance if number two holds up. Maybe God will be on our side."

Jim turned to his copilot, "Bill, could you take over for a while? My legs are about to give out. I think we'll have to trade off more often."

"Sure thing."

They had stopped losing altitude for now at least. Jim relaxed a bit, for the first time since the bomb run. He knew they were still in deadly danger. That damaged engine could give out at any time.

Things were not going so good with the ball turret gunner, Milton Finkenstadt. He'd had an accident in his flight suit and the smell was nauseating. He thought he'd throw up.

He yelled back at his buddy, "Hey Herb, can you hear me?"

"Whatcha want? For Chris sake, I was half asleep."

"I had an accident in my suit. What'll I do? I can't stand this mess."

"What'll you do? You stupid asshole. You'll just sit there and do your duty, whatever Cap says."

"I thought we were buddies."

"We are, but you come up with some of the most asinine questions."

"Give me a break, I'm only nineteen, you know."

"What's that got to do with it? I'm only twenty. Get your act together. If anybody can get us through, it's Captain Scott."

"Do you think we'll ever make it? I heard the other night some of the groups have lost more than fifty per cent. I was never meant to be a soldier. I'm just a civilian masquerading as a G.I."

"You and millions of others. I sure hope we make it. I've got this hot chick I met at the plant. She's all I can think about."

"You can think about sex at a time like this?"

"I guess it's a talent."

Milt said, "I'm sending most of my pay to Mom and Dad. His business is way off. Guess he's getting old. Miss them a lot."

"Could you shut up for a while? I'm gonna take a nap. Let me know if anything happens."

"I can't believe you can take a nap now."

"Well I am. Knock it off, will you?"

Up in the cockpit, Jim was somewhat encouraged. So far number two was holding up.

"How's the oil pressure on two?"

Bill checked the gage, "It's down slightly but I think it's stabilized. There isn't that much smoke now."

Just then the navigator came on, "Captain, we're now over Holland. We should head for the Zuider Zee, then cross the channel."

"Roger."

Bill was still sweating it out, "We might make it even if we have to bail out. I've heard the Dutch have a strong underground. I've never liked the idea of getting shot hanging in a chute."

Losing all patience, Jim raised his voice, "Me either! For Christ's sake can't you think of something cheerful to talk about?"

After this Bill decided to keep his big mouth shut. He was getting testy.

Back in the ball turret, Milton Findenstadt had been able to clean up a bit. "Herb, did you know I'm a volunteer?"

"You jerk, you woke me up. I thought you were drafted like everybody else."

For once he was one up on his friend. "When I heard what that bastard Hitler was doing to the Jews, I just had to sign up. Basically, I'm a peace-loving kind of guy."

"Me too! You didn't look too peaceful when you shot down a couple of those M.E. 109's."

"I just pretend they're Hitler, not some nice young German boy like you or me."

"That's the way."

"I'd hate to shoot somebody in cold blood looking them right in the eye."

"You know what they say about war? It's just a bunch of old guys getting young fellas killed."

"That's probably right, but what could Roosevelt do? The Nazis were taking over Europe and England was about to collapse. Then the Japs hit Pearl Harbor. I think he's a great man."

Up in front, the deathly silence was marred only by the droning of the engines. They were over the blue expanse of the Zuider Zee. The pressure was dropping again on two. Bill knew it couldn't hold up long, regardless of what Jim said. Watching it go down, he secretly said a prayer.

Suddenly, the ill fated ship started to shake perilously.

Jim yelled on the intercom, "What's going on back there? There's more black smoke. Bill, change the mixture on two. Maybe that'll help."

"Too late, the pressure's dropping like a rock. It's failing for sure."

Finkenstadt shouted, "It's on fire."

"Feather two! Hit the extinguisher!" Jim yelled.

Bill hit the switch. Jim moved the throttles to full power on the two remaining engines, but it was a losing battle. They were losing altitude fast. "Give me a hand. Maybe we can steady it a bit until we get out. We'll have to bail out."

They strained with all their strength and were just able, momentarily, to stop it from going into a spin. They turned to get back over the land.

Sighting what looked like solid ground below, Captain Scott went on the horn one final time. "Listen you guys. It's over now; we've got to bail out. Wait for the signal. Number two is out and the other two are failing. Remember your training. Jump clear of the ship, count to ten, and pull the ripcord. Flex your knees when you hit so you absorb the impact. Bury your chute as fast as you can and head for cover. The resistance should see you, but the Germans may also, so be prepared. Good luck." He opened the bomb bay doors hoping for the best. They listened to the eerie sound as the doors ground slowly open.

The doomsday scenario. The remaining two engines failed. The ominous silence was deafening. All they could hear was the wind whistling through the stricken ship. Jim checked below. Now they were definitely over solid land.

He yelled, "JUMP!" on the intercom. There was no reply from the crew but he assumed they had gotten safely away.

"Now Bill, you go."

Drawing on courage he didn't know he had, Bill said, "You go first, I'll try to steady her."

Jim angrily shouted, "I'm still in charge here. Out you go. Be quick about it." He watched as Bill's chute opened and he drifted safely down.

In his last act on the doomed ship, Jim put on the auto pilot, hoping that it might do some good. He jumped free pulling the ripcord just at the right time. It was like a frozen moment in time as he floated down. He was horrified when the ship went into a full spin and headed straight for him. He was barely able to maneuver out of its path and watched as it crashed with a loud explosion and started to burn. He thought if that didn't rouse the Germans nothing would.

CHAPTER III

"Don't make a peep."

Jim hit the ground hard in an open area, shaken up, but unhurt. He scrambled to corral the chute and bury it. Scanning the area, there wasn't a sign of the enemy or his crew. He ran to the nearest thicket of trees and found cover. Just as he entered the woods, he spotted a group of civilians approaching across the field in his direction. Crouching down, he drew his pistol, fearing the worst.

As they approached, a tall blond Hollander dressed in civvies, flashed a broad smile, and called out in fluent English, "Welcome, Yank, put your gun away, you're safe now."

"Who are you?"

"Nels Maas of the Dutch underground sir, we're here to help you."

Jim exhaled, grinning, "That's good news."

Nels introduced his colleagues who greeted Jim warmly, even if he couldn't understand them.

"We've got to get you out of here on the double. The Germans have patrols out and they might of seen you. They couldn't have missed the explosion."

"I'm in your hands." He couldn't believe his good fortune in being found so quickly.

"Quick, change out of your uniform and we'll bury it. Here are some clothes you can wear." He handed over a pair of well worn trousers and a heavy gray wool sweater. Jim quickly changed, as the rest of the party disappeared into the woods, happy to get out of that area.

"Follow me, Captain, be quick about it. I just heard the sound of a motorcycle on the road nearby. One more thing, if we should be stopped, you're deaf and dumb. Don't say a thing. I'll handle it."

Nels took off in a dog trot with Jim right behind. They ran for about a mile, when Nels stopped and pulled some branches aside to reveal two bicycles carefully hidden in the bushes.

"Captain, can you ride a bike?"

Breathing deeply, "Can I? Since I was seven."

They mounted and set off rapidly down a path to a paved road, and once on the pavement, pedaled even faster toward some unknown destination. For the first time since he was a boy, Jim was totally dependent on another man, one he didn't even know. For a self-reliant combat veteran it was a new experience. Barely able to keep up with the younger man, he was too winded to exchange a word. Visibility was partially obscured by the fog, and they rode in comparative safety for a half hour. As they came to the top of a rise Jim could barely make out a farm house they seemed to be headed toward.

Nels pulled into the gravel driveway of the old stone building and dismounted. Walking to the door, he turned to Jim, "The owner of this farm is one of our loyal supporters. We should be safe here. We'll rest up and get a bite to eat. When it's dark, we'll head for town. That'll take at least an hour."

Still puffing, "I could stand some rest. It's been a long day. We took off from England very early and completed our mission successfully bombing an airplane plant in Hamburg. We were hit right after and struggled back to Holland hoping to get back to England. The engines gave out and we had to bail out."

"How many of you were there?"

"Nine men. Did you hear any news about the others?"

"Not yet. They're probably all right. I don't have a radio."

"Where, exactly, are we?"

"You just came into land off the Zuider Zee. You've heard of that?"

"My navigator told me about it. The only thing I know for sure, I'm in Holland."

"After we rest up a bit I'll take you into the small town of Groot. We have a safe house there owned by a nice lady that hates the Nazis with a passion. You can stay there until we can get you out of the country or the war's over. It's a little old farming community."

Jim was a little reassured. "Why can't we just stay here? Wouldn't it be easier?"

"You'll see. The farmer's very old and can barely take care of himself. His wife died. It wouldn't be safe here for long. The Germans check out these farm houses regularly."

"Just tell me what to do. Believe me; I appreciate what you're doing. Let's cut out this captain stuff. I go by Jim."

"You bet, as they say in America. It'll be Jim from now on."

As Nels started to knock, they heard the sound of a motorcycle in the distance.

"Hurry Yank. Follow me."

He hastily led the way to an old stone barn that looked like it'd been there forever. Nels forced open the rusty barn door and they hid their bikes in a stall. The farmer had milk cows. Jim could make out stanchions at one end of the barn. Just then they heard the motorcycle pull up in front of the farmhouse.

Peeking through a crack in the door, Nels whispered, "It's a German all right. He's obviously looking for survivors from the crash. Here, bury yourself in the hay and don't make a peep."

Jim hurriedly complied, whispering, "What'll they do if they catch us?"

"We'll be shot on the spot, you as a spy and me as a traitor. Now keep quiet." Jim didn't have any difficulty obeying that command.

A young fair haired German trooper pounded angrily on the front door, and, after a long wait, a light went on in back and the owner opened the door a crack. Jim heard them talking loudly in Dutch, but couldn't understand the language. It didn't sound too friendly but it did seem like they had come to some kind of an agreement.

Jim whispered to Nels, "What'd they say?"

"I heard the farmer say he heard the crash of a large airplane. He thinks the crew all died in the bay."

"Did he believe him?"

"I don't know. We'll find out shortly."

The front door slammed and the trooper walked over toward the barn. Jim felt beads of sweat on his forehead. The German stopped in front of the barn door looking perplexed, studying the door, which they'd failed to close all the way. Jim drew his pistol, gripping it tightly, hoping he wouldn't have to use it. The trooper started to enter the barn, shining his flashlight around, when the farmer rushed out of the house.

He yelled, "Corporal! Corporal! Here's some coffee for you." He held up a large mug of steaming coffee. The Nazi turned and walked back toward the house, obviously pleased at the offer. It had been a long, hard day on patrol and he welcomed the break. Jim breathed a sigh of relief. He never was that good of a shot. The thought of shooting the German boy point blank appalled him.

Finishing the coffee, the trooper mounted his motorbike and rode off in the distance. The newfound friends happily brushed the hay off and walked over to the farmhouse. The farmer had bolted the door, perhaps concerned that the Nazi might return, not sure if they were still out there.

Nels pounded on the heavy door. Between knocks, he explained, "That trooper is with the regular army. They're not too bad. Not like the Gestapo. The worst of all are those from the occupied countries. They know Germany is losing the war and they won't have any place to go back to, and they certainly can't stay here."

After a bit, the heavy wooden door squeaked open a crack and the farmer peered apprehensively out. When the owner, Willem Brinkerhoff, recognized Nels, he threw the door open and greeted him warmly. He was an old man, squat but solidly built, his face wrinkled by long years working in the sun. He escorted them into the cold musty room illuminated by a single candle. There was a small wood fire on the hearth that hardly affected the dampness.

Nels introduced Jim to the farmer in Dutch. He could barely make out the meaning.

"Yank, rest here, by the fire." The farmer motioned to a well worn easy chair. Nels and the farmer sat down at a crude wooden table in straight back chairs and started to talk in Dutch. Jim collapsed in the beat-up old chair, limp as a dish rag. He realized he'd been functioning on adrenaline most of the day, the classic emergency reaction. With the warmth of the fire, and the conversation he didn't understand, he quickly dozed off, relaxed and warmed by the fire.

After several hours of recuperative sleep, he woke with a start. The two countrymen were still talking. Thinking about the events of the day, he was still worried about the crew, wondering if they had got down all right. He was glad he didn't have to use the gun.

Nels noticed that he was awake, "Jim you should get up now. Are you feeling any better? We'll eat something and be off."

Seated around the rustic table, their genial host, who seemed to welcome the company, served steaming bowls of a hearty potato soup with coarse homemade brown bread and mugs of hot coffee, which they wolfed down.

Jim said, "Does he know what happened with the other men from my ship?"

"Mr. Brinkerhoff heard they landed in the bay just short of land. Several small boats headed out to pick them up. They're probably all right."

"Thank God for that. And another thing, how'd he know we were hiding in the barn?"

"His dog barked when we came up. He knew it wasn't the Germans."

"We're lucky for his quick thinking. I hope you told him how much we appreciate what he did."

"I sure did. Luck plays only a small role in our operations. Mostly, it's good planning and execution, but in this case, I'd have to agree, luck played a part."

"I still wonder what happened to my copilot, Lieutenant Richter. He's younger than me, about six foot, brown eyed and good looking. He bailed out just before I did. I saw his chute open."

"One of your lads landed on solid ground. They saw him land, but couldn't get to him in time. He disappeared into the woods. He should be all right. They've probably found him by now."

What a strange turn of events this was. He had only a couple of missions and he would have gone home. Here he was, in an ancient stone farmhouse in the low country of Holland beholden to Nels, a young Dutchman he hardly knew. Literally, his life was in his hands. But he was fortunate to still be alive.

Jim had a chance to study his protector. Nels Maas was a tall, fair-haired and wiry Dutchman who looked like he would be barely out of high school in the states. It was hard to believe how courageous and tough he was when push came to shove.

"Nels, could you tell me a little more about the resistance?"

"We're well organized and have groups all around the country. We don't have a lot of money but several wealthy businessmen are secretly helping us. Our main objectives are to rescue allied airmen down over our territory and espionage. We've set up a network of safe houses and have wide support from the people. Most of the citizens hate the Nazis. They've taken over our country, pillaged our crops and livestock and rape our women."

"What were you doing before the war?"

"I was at university, studying for the bar, like my father. He was a barrister."

"Do you think I can get back to my outfit? I'd like to get back to England. I already feel like a shirker."

"Forget that. You've done your part. We'll get you to that safe house. You might be there for the duration. You never know, our leadership might work something out."

By the light of the flickering candle, Nels had a chance to study his charge. Jim Scott was rather boyish in appearance, tall, dark eyed, with ready intelligence. He seemed hardened by all the missions and good in tough spots, but he was obviously out of shape.

Nels said, "We'll have to move on shortly. We'll walk to Groot, it's about ten miles. We better not take the bikes tonight. Some of the other guys might need them. We should be all right on this dark night. We'll hide the bikes here if we need them in the future. We'll have to get out of the way if we encounter anybody, which is unlikely this late at night. Just remember, if we do, you're deaf and dumb. Let me do the talking. While we have wide support you can never tell. There are collaborators you can't trust. It'll take an hour or two. Have you had enough to eat?"

"I'm fine. I'm ready when you are."

Nels got up, turned to Willem, and gave him a bear hug. Jim jumped up, thanked the old farmer in English, shook his roughened hand and clapped him on the back. Nels led the way as they slipped silently out into the uncertain night. The sky was overcast with little visibility. Jim knew he'd have to stay tight to the Dutch lad or he'd lose the way. Nels started off at a brisk pace with the American close behind. Even with the Air Force calisthenics, he had difficulty keeping up with the young Dutchman.

After walking a while, he asked, between breaths, "This work you do, it's got to be terribly dangerous."

"You're probably right, but it's something I've got to do. It's our only way of getting back at them. You know, we're a little country, ill-prepared for the attack in 1942. We didn't have a chance. It's real bad here. You ought to see what they're doing to the Jews. They make them wear this big Star of David badge. They're persecuting them."

"I don't know much about that. Some people back home think they brought it on themselves, since they're so rich and all."

"Is that what Americans think?"

"I don't know about that."

"Listen, Captain, let's talk about this some other time. Save your breath. We've a long way yet."

Nels quickened the pace and Jim struggled to keep up.

"What's that? Did you hear something?" Nels motioned to stop walking and be quiet. They could just barely hear the muffled sound of an engine coming in their direction. To Nels' practiced ear, it was clearly a German lorry. They were usually the only ones on the road at that time of night.

"Quick, follow me." He led off the road to a deep ditch, partially filled with water. They huddled on the wet ground. Jim started to shake with the cold and wet seeping into his clothes. Then they could discern the headlights of the vehicle. Jim held his breath, watching as the lorry passed. Four young German soldiers were clearly visible, sitting at attention, with guns at the ready.

As they watched the vehicle disappeared in the dark, Jim breathed a sigh of relief, "They sure have a lot of patrols out at night."

"They do at that. I think they know we are active around here. I'm sure they heard the explosion when your plane hit the ground, so they're probably redoubling their efforts."

Scrambling out of the ditch, Nels started off again at even a faster pace. As they rounded a bend in the road, Jim could barely make out some lights and the shape of some buildings in the distance.

"Now we've got to be extra careful. That's Groot up ahead. We'll slip from house to house. Most of the residents support us, but you can never tell. As I told you, we have these traitorous collaborators."

He led the way, running from house to house, finding safety in the darkness. Jim was close behind, confident of Nels' knowledge of the town. Peering out from behind an old stone cottage Jim whispered to Nels, but he shushed him, and motioned for him to follow. They quickly set off again, careful to stay in the shadows. When they reached the end of the street Nels paused, carefully surveyed the quiet neighborhood, and cautiously approached the darkened door of one of the smallest houses.

CHAPTER IV

"Shaking involuntarily, he broke out in a cold sweat."

Bill Richter had a difficult landing, barely avoiding the swirling waters of the Zuider Zee. As he struggled to unfasten his chute, which was billowing in the wind, he felt a stabbing pain in his right ankle. It had been injured when he hit the ground. Remembering the captain's last minute instructions, he hurried to bury the chute and survey the surroundings. No one was in sight. It was low land, probably reclaimed from the sea. He spotted a hedgerow and rushed to find cover in the bushes. His movements were impeded by his now swollen ankle. Safely screened and secure for the moment, he fell to the ground, done in by the dangers he had faced and the effort of limping on his painful ankle.

Where were the resistance fighters he had counted on? He had neglected to put a map of Holland in his flight suit. Here he was in a strange country all alone without a map or anyone to help him. Shaking involuntarily, he broke out in a cold sweat. As a boy he had always used sleep as a way to escape adversity. Once again it worked for him. He fell fast asleep on the cold ground and, for a time, forgot all of his troubles. When he came to several hours later he collected his thoughts and was able to think more rationally about his situation. Actually, he was fortunate to be alive and reasonably well, except for his sore ankle. He had his Colt 45, a compass and a packet of K rations. As the sun set in the west he resolved to set out the next day in the hope of finding the underground, or at least a friendly farmer who might help him.

At the break of dawn the rising sun warmed his aching body. He struggled to regain consciousness, quickly recalling his dire predicament. He ate several K rations and washed them down with a swig from his canteen. Heartened by the fair weather and the nourishment, he set off across the fields determined to make the most of a difficult situation. Using his compass for guidance he headed due east away from the sea. The main thing was to avoid capture and becoming a prisoner of war. It was his sworn duty to evade the enemy. He had been briefed that the Dutch hated the Nazis and the occupation. Perhaps he could find help.

He hiked the better part of that first day, stopping only to rest occasionally, or to relieve himself. It was slow going, despite his best efforts, with the wet soil and his painful ankle. Late in the day he spotted a windmill that was used to pump water for irrigation. He found shelter that night in the creaking structure, out of the wind and the chill. He slept well, happy to be off of the cold ground. The next day he set out again. His ankle had swollen even more and he suffered cruelly from the throbbing pain. Late in the afternoon he made out a small stone farmhouse in the distance. He had to risk it. He couldn't walk much further with his injury. With every step in the sodden earth the pain grew more intense. Dragging his injured leg he arrived at the door of the farmhouse. Perhaps this Dutch farmer would help an American airman. If he was a collaborator it would be all over. Maybe now, even being taken prisoner would be better than trying to go on, which seemed all but impossible. He pounded repeatedly on the heavy door but to no avail. When he was about to give up he spotted an elderly farmer carrying a bucket of milk coming out of the stone barn.

Bill called out, "Hello! Hello there!"

With no sign of recognition, he yelled louder, "Hey there! Hello!" He started in the direction of the barn.

Finally, the grizzled old man looked up and saw him. He shouted in broken English, "Who are ya? Whatcha doing here?" He hurried over to confront the stranger.

As he approached, he made out Bill's flight suit and insignia. "Yur a Yank! You're welcome here. Come in, rest yourself."

Bill struggled to follow him into his home, dragging his right leg behind him, where he plopped down in a soft chair offered by his host. Without a further word he fell asleep, certain that he had found sanctuary in this humble abode. At last he felt he had a chance and was in helpful hands.

CHAPTER V

"Captain, you're welcome here"

May 18th, 1944, Groot, Holland

When they arrived at the safe house, Nels cautiously knocked on the heavy wooden door, trying to keep the sound to a minimum. They waited and waited. He rapped again louder. After repeated efforts, the door opened a crack and a middle aged woman peered out.

Recognizing Nels, she beamed and threw the door open. "Nels, it's you. Come in, my friend." She gave him a bear hug.

They followed her in and she shut and carefully bolted the door. Jim looked her over, knowing that he'd be spending time with her in this house. She was short, full bodied, but not fat, with a plain round face, her white hair bound tightly in a bun at the top of her head. She looked about fifty. Her blue eyes sparkled with maternal warmth and vitality. The two Hollanders talked rapidly in Dutch. Jim surmised that Nels was telling her about his rescue and the subsequent events leading up to their arrival at her doorstep.

At last they noticed him. "Jim, I want you to meet Gretel Ruyschel. She's owner of this house. She'll be looking after you. She also has a friend who lives with her, Jacob Schimmel."

Jim shook hands with Gretel, who, to his surprise, greeted him in broken English. He felt fortunate that she spoke English.

"Captain Scott, welcome. Food's scarce, but we sort of get along with the help of the underground."

"It's so good of you to take me in. It's got to be dangerous for you and your friend."

"It's the least we can do. Our only hope is the Americans and the British. One day we'll get our homeland back from this Nazi curse."

Suddenly, a large black rottweiller charged Jim out of the darkness in the hallway growling and snarling ferociously.

He stepped back, screening himself behind Nels, who seemed unconcerned by all of this.

Gretel's face reddened. She yelled, "Fang, Fang, sit down!"

The black dog reluctantly obeyed, still growling menacingly.

"Don't worry, he doesn't bite. He's a good watch dog though."

Jim still didn't trust the dog, who obviously didn't like him. He stayed a step behind Nels, wishing he could give it a good kick.

She led the way into a small gloomy parlor furnished in old, dark overstuffed furniture. Just as they sat down a large imposing figure of a man, probably in his early fifties, entered the room. He had a fixed frown on his otherwise handsome face. Tall, with only a touch of gray, he looked the picture of good health. Even in the circumstances, he had an air of affluence about him and an aristocratic bearing.

Gretel rose to introduce him, "Captain Scott, this is my friend, Jacob Schimmel. He'll be living here until the war's over. He lost his business to the Nazis in Amsterdam. Came back here to his home town to find shelter. His family lived in this neighborhood years ago."

Jim stood up, offering his hand, "Glad to meet you, Mr. Schimmel." He turned away to avoid shaking hands.

Jim had always prided himself on being able to get along with anyone, but this might be a challenge. He obviously didn't want him there. Jim knew his presence could be a serious danger to the residents of this house, so he could, in part at least, understand Jacob's attitude.

As the three countrymen lapsed into animated conversation in Dutch, Jim studied the room carefully, knowing that he could be spending long months in this humble home. Poorly illuminated by a kerosene lantern with no discernable heat, the room was bone cold and dank. On the walls were old family photographs. It was apparent from the furniture and the pictures that the house had seen better days.

Schimmel stood up and disappeared to the back of the house, without another word to Jim. Gretel led the way back to the large kitchen with its rough stone floor. Illuminated more adequately, and warmed by an ancient cook stove, it seemed cheerful compared to the front parlor.

They sat down on sturdy kitchen chairs close to the warmth. Gretel turned to Jim, "Captain, would you like some coffee?"

"Sure would. Thank you. Listen, let's drop the formalities. I go by Jim. All my friends call me Jim."

Blushing, "I'll try to remember that. It'll be Jim from now on."

She took a heavy iron coffee pot off the stove, retrieved three brown pottery mugs from the cupboard, and poured out strong black coffee for each of them. Jacob was nowhere in sight.

"Would you like a little something to eat?"

"Thank you."

She found a loaf of coarse brown bread in another cupboard and carefully cut three slices of precisely the same size, one for each of them, and three small wedges of well-aged Gouda cheese.

Jim sipped the strong black coffee, grimacing at its potency. He knew that Europeans preferred strong coffee, but this was the strongest he'd ever tasted. The bread was good; obviously home-made, and the cheese outstanding. But no seconds were offered.

Gretel found it fascinating to sit there and visit with an American aviator. "Captain, where do you come from in the states?"

"I grew up in Concord, Massachusetts. You know, Boston is in Massachusetts. You may have heard of Boston."

"Wasn't Massachusetts one of the original colonies?"

"That's right, Gretel, do you mind if I call you by your first name?"

"Not at all."

"Wasn't there a famous battle there during the Revolutionary War?"

"You're right, ma'am." Jim was amazed at her knowledge of the states when he knew practically nothing about Holland. All he ever thought of was windmills and tulips. "Have you ever been to the states?"

"When I was very young. It was a wonderful trip. My father took me, but we only visited New York."

Nels listened intently, wondering how they would get along. Time was getting short, "Listen Jim. I've got to get going. I need to tell you some things. The Germans conduct regular patrols in Groot and make random searches of a few of the houses. Lately, they've stepped up their efforts. It's obvious they know we've been rescuing some allied airmen."

"How do they know that?"

"It's pretty simple. They've seen many parachutes come down, and, with our efforts, they've only captured a few."

"What happened to those they've captured?"

"It all depends. If they're still in uniform we presume they take them to a prisoner of war camp."

"What happens if they're out of uniform?"

"They're probably shot as spies."

"Have any been shot?"

"We're not sure, but we believe some have."

Nels got up and walked over to the side of the room next to a built-in wooden bench. Reaching underneath at the side, he located a hidden latch that secured the seat. He unfastened the latch and raised the seat.

"Here Jim, take a look at this." Jim moved over, and peered down into the darkness below.

Nels shone his flashlight into the space. Jim could just make out a skillfully concealed tunnel under the house. It looked gloomy and dank down there, but obviously it was a good place for anyone hiding from the Nazis. The latch was well hidden and there were even the heads of nails making it appear that the seat was securely nailed down. When it was latched, you couldn't budge it.

"It's not too pleasant down there, sort of damp and musty, but it should be quite safe in case of an inspection. There are some matches and a candle for light. If a German patrol comes to the front door, you get down there real fast. Take all your things with you. You must keep your clothing and personal effects in the kitchen ready for concealment. As you well know, this isn't some little game, but a life or death business. It could make all the difference for you and Gretel. Usually, you'll hear them up the street so you'll have time."

"I see what you mean. Wasn't it difficult to dig a tunnel like that?"

"Not really. You may have noticed, the land around here is very low, and the houses are built up about four feet, so it didn't take that much digging. We just spread the dirt around down there. There's plenty of room to sit comfortably but you can't stand up."

"Sure looks like you've thought of everything. My hat's off to you."

Jim wondered what would happen if they searched the building. His admiration for the resistance was growing. He climbed down into the crude tunnel to check it out, wondering what the mold would do to his allergies. The only problem he could see was the latch had to be fastened from the outside. If Gretel was at the door trying to stall the Nazis, Jacob would have to take care of the latch. Maybe he'd just have to hope for the best if that happened, but he still thought he could win him over. Nels had said they could usually hear them up the street so there was time.

"I've got to get going. The moon is under a cloud, a good time to get out of town." Nels said.

"I can't thank you enough Nels, for all you've done for me."

"It's all for a good cause. I'll stop by one of these nights to see how you're doing. Don't mind Jacob too much. He does take a bit of getting used to."

Nels slipped quietly out of the back door into the darkness. Jim faced adjustment to his new living arrangements, but was thankful for his good luck.

"Say, Captain. I'll get another chair for you." Gretel walked into the front room and returned with an ancient wooden rocker and sat it close to the fire.

"This'll be more comfortable."

Jim couldn't believe how considerate she was. All the other chairs had straight backs and a hard seat while the rocker had a cushion.

"Why don't you take the rocker?" he asked.

"No, it's for you."

She was tired after all of the events of the day. "Well, Captain, it's only eleven but we go to bed early now. Jacob's probably already asleep. You can sit up here if you want, but I better show you your room first."

"I won't be sitting up. It's been a long day. I'm ready for bed." He thought of their early morning take off in England and all of the events that had transpired since. He wondered, once more, how the rest of the crew had fared, but he had been reassured by what the farmer had said. Gretel picked up the kerosene lamp and led the way down a dark hallway to a small bedroom at the side of the house.

"We converted it from a garage. That's why it has a concrete floor."

With no heat and the concrete floor, it was cold as a tomb. Furnished sparsely with a simple iron bedstead and a small bureau with a mirror, it was still a welcome sight for Jim, who hadn't been in a bed since he left England. It seemed like an eternity, but he had only taken off that morning.

"There's some soap and water on the bureau if you want to wash up. Tomorrow I'll find you some more suitable clothes. The facilities are out back, if you need to go. It's what you Americans call an outhouse. Those damned Germans cut off our water supply and electricity, but we have a well. The only heat is in the kitchen. Jacob scrounges around the countryside to keep us supplied with firewood."

Jim thought maybe Jacob had some good points after all.

"Good night Gretel, thanks again."

"The bed does have some warm wool blankets so you should be all right. Good night." She quietly closed the door, groping through the darkened house to get to bed herself, having left the lamp behind for him.

He pulled his dirty flight boots off and climbed into bed fully clothed, pulling the warm blankets over his frigid body. He was out instantly and slept straight through until the first light of day, awakened by an urgent need to pee. He gingerly stepped out of bed onto the cold floor, pulled his boots on, and felt his way down the hall in the semi-darkness and located the door outside, where he spotted the primitive stone outhouse. It reminded him of summers on his grandfather's farm in Vermont. It had two round necessary holes and some old newspapers for sanitation. The stench was overpowering, but it would serve the purpose. He relieved himself, went back to the bedroom, washed his hands and face in the cold water and went over to the kitchen where he encountered Jacob and Gretel warming by the fire.

Gretel stood up, "Good morning Captain, come sit by the fire. It's cold and windy outside."

"Good morning ma'am and Mr. Schimeel."

Jacob grunted an unrecognizable answer. The black dog was sleeping peacefully on a knotted rug near the stove.

"Here, take this chair." She pulled the rocker closer to the fire. "I'll collect some clothes and toilet articles in town. How'd you like the outhouse? Did you ever see anything like that?"

"I have. When I was a boy, I used to spend summers on grandfather's farm in Vermont. When we were dirty from working in the fields, grandmother used to make us use it."

"Was it a nice farm?"

"Sure was, about a hundred acres. Had a pretty white clapboard farmhouse and red barns, just like a picture. Grandpa had a nice herd of Jersey milk cows, sort of like you have here."

Jacob sniffed contemptuously. Gretel either was unaware of his attitude or just chose to ignore it. What a strange pair they were. Jacob was tall, handsome and muscular. She was short and dumpy, with a prominent nose. With her hausfrau manner, she nonetheless, projected warmth and sincerity. Jacob never uttered a civil word, at least to Jim. He obviously resented his presence in the house.

"Did you sleep well?" She asked.

"Like a log, slept straight through 'til morning."

"That's good. I'm sure you needed it. Maybe, some time you could tell me about your mission and how you happened to land in Holland."

"When you have time."

"How about something to eat?"

"That'd be great."

Gretel poured a steaming mug of black coffee and handed him two large hard rolls.

"I'm afraid this is all we have this morning. We've been on short rations. There's nothing much to buy in town but usually the resistance helps us out. We should be getting some supplies this week."

"This'll do just fine, ma'am. I'm not too hungry anyway." It was a little white lie, but he didn't dare tell her how hungry he really was.

"Would you like another cup?"

"No, I've had plenty."

"Starting tomorrow we'll have breakfast at eight o'clock sharp. Will that be all right with you?"

"I'll be ready."

"If you'll excuse me now? I've got to tend to my chores."

After she left, Jim hesitantly ventured conversation with Jacob. "Did you sleep well?"

"I did."

"What do you do during the day?"

He flushed, "That's none of your business."

The atmosphere in the kitchen settled into a pattern of strained silence. The flames danced cheerily. Jim contented himself staring into the fire. Jacob fell asleep, snoring loudly. It was peaceful but boring. He was lucky not to be in a prisoner of war camp, or worse. He'd have to figure out some way to make himself useful to pass the time. With nothing to read and no one to talk to during the day it could be a problem.

After a meager lunch of cabbage soup and bread, and a skimpy dinner, Jim was hungry all the time. He dreamed that night of a large steak and baked potato dinner at one of his favorite spots in Boston. He slept soundly, though, thankful for the warm blankets in the frigid room. He woke up promptly at six thirty, as was his military custom, and washed his body down with the towel and cold water. Shivering, he hurried to dress, and suffered through the onerous task of visiting the outdoor privy, which was even colder than his room. He hurried back to the warmth of the kitchen where Gretel was sipping her coffee. The rottweiler dozed peacefully on the rug. Hearing Jim approach, it jumped into Jim's rocker. When Jim tried to coax him out, the dog growled menacingly. He avoided a confrontation by sitting in one of the hard chairs which he pulled up by the fire. He decided to bide his time and deal with the rotten dog when nobody was around. He'd figure something out. For breakfast they had the same meal as the first day, black coffee and hard rolls.

Jim asked, "When do you think we'll see Nels again?"

"I really don't know. They're very secretive." Gretel said.

Jacob looked distinguished, with tan trousers, carefully creased, and a red wool sweater. His mustache was immaculately trimmed.

Jim made another stab at conversation. "How're things going with you?" Jacob acted like his privacy had been invaded, mumbling, "All right, I guess."

"Well that's good to hear. What do you have planned for the day?"

Jacob ignored the question, refusing to answer.

Jacob turned to Gretel, "When are we going to get some fruit and vegetables?"

"I don't know, dear. Nels and the lads are doing their best. The Germans take everything, but he promised to bring some supplies soon."

"We'd do a lot better if we were friendlier with the Nazis."

"Why, Jacob, what a terrible thing to say."

"I was only kidding, don't get upset."

Jim avoided an argument by remaining quiet. He wondered how much Jacob was to be trusted. Now was a good time to visit the outhouse again.

One week later, on a dark and blustery night, sitting in the kitchen, they heard a soft rap on the back door. The back yard was screened by a stone wall. Gretel jumped right up, recognizing the knock, and let Nels in. He looked disheveled and tired.

"Why Nels, you look sort of done in. Are you all right?"

"Sure, I am. We were out all night on an assignment. I'm a little tired. Here's some things for you that may help out."

He handed over a large basket laden with bread, cheese, some cabbages and a few apples.

Gretel smiled broadly. Even Jacob looked pleased. "My word, Nels, this is wonderful. How can we thank you?"

"It's from our farmer friend, Willem Brinkerhoff. You'll remember him Jim."

"I sure do. I'll be eternally in his debt."

Gretel looked puzzled, "How do you know him, Captain?"

"Well, ma'am, it was like this. After Nels picked me up down near the water, we bicycled to his farm to rest and get some food. Just after we got there, we heard a German motorcycle coming up the road. We hid in the barn in the hay mow. This soldier dismounted, talked to the farmer, and walked over to the barn, like he was going to search it. We'd rushed and left the door ajar. Apparently, Mr. Brinkerhoff knew we were out there. He came out just at the opportune time and distracted that Nazi with coffee and conversation. He convinced him that I'd probably gone down in the water. After drinking the coffee and talking a while, he took off on his motorcycle. You can see why I said that farmer saved my neck. I had a gun but didn't want to use it."

"How'd he know you were out there?"

"He told us later that his dog barked when we came up and he assumed we must be hidden in the barn. He'd heard the plane crash and thought there were survivors."

"That was quick thinking on his part."

"Sure was."

"And now he sends all this food."

"He hates the Nazis with a passion. His only son was killed fighting during the invasion in '42." Nels added.

Gretel busied herself putting the supplies away, smiling at their good fortune. Jim thought it was the first time he'd seen her looking so happy since he'd got there.

When she finished, she turned to Jacob, "And now we should leave these two alone so they can talk. Let's go into the front parlor."

"But, Gretel, it's cold in there."

"Now dear, it'll be all right. You can cover up with that wool wrap on the couch."

With a dirty look, he reluctantly followed her into the parlor.

Nels relaxed a bit, "Jim, it's good to see you in some decent clothes. How've you been getting along?"

"Gretel found these pants and sweater in town somehow. She's amazing, always calm and good natured. She's been wonderful to me. In the face of all this danger, she just goes about her daily housework like nothing's happened. I figure down deep she's tough as nails. But Jacob, that's another story."

"What about Jacob?"

"What's he doing here anyway?"

"He was a successful businessman before the war. Made a lot of money importing goods from the Far East. You know, textiles, pottery and the like. When the Krauts came they seized all his assets. He and his partner had some ships and a large warehouse in Amsterdam. He's broke, but thinks he's above all of us. Sometimes he talks like a Nazi sympathizer, but that doesn't make sense, after what happened to his business. They knew each other growing up here years ago. When her husband was killed by the

Germans, she needed a man, I guess. Anyway they got together. She's been taking care of him ever since."

"Are they married?"

"No, they're not. Common law you'd call it in the states."

"I think she's been taken in. She loves him, that's for sure, but I think he's just using her."

"I try not to judge other people's relationships."

"A real son of a bitch."

"You might be right."

"What a story, stranger than fiction. Some day I'd like to write all this up, the German occupation of the Netherlands and all. It would be part of the history of the war and the Dutch resistance."

"What a great idea. Listen, my friend, I've got to get going. It's getting late. Don't forget what I told you about the patrols. You can never be too careful."

"I've heard them a couple of times already, but they didn't stop here."

Nels stood up and clasped Jim's hand, "Goodbye for now. I'll be around again, but it'll be a while. We're going out on a special mission next week. Don't mention it to Gretel or Jacob. The fewer people who know the better."

"Good luck."

He slipped quietly out the back door into the dark night. Jim's admiration knew no bounds. This young man, not yet twenty one, risked his life in a noble cause. He felt a little guilty safely settled here while his comrades in the Eighth were still risking their necks daily over Germany.

CHAPTER VI

"If he was caught helping the airman, it'd be all over for him."

May, 1944; a farmhouse in the countryside of Holland

After a long night's sleep in the arm chair, Bill struggled to regain consciousness. For a time he couldn't get his bearings. Temporarily disoriented, slowly it came back to him. He had found his way to this farm and the friendly old owner had offered to help him. He felt refreshed after the sound sleep, but his right ankle throbbed with pain. The slight strain he'd experienced when he hit the ground had been aggravated by his two-day trek to find shelter. The details of his arrival there and meeting with the owner were still a blur in his mind.

The farmer saw that he was stirring, "Yank, you're awake. How do ya feel?"

"I'm all right. It's just that my ankle hurts like hell. I injured it when I hit the ground back there by the Zuider Zee. I'm afraid I've made it worse getting here. Could you tell me your name again? I'm afraid I forgot."

"Jan. Jan Cortsandt. What's yours?"

"I go by Bill, Bill Richter."

"Heard some of your boys had been coming down over the homeland."

"That's pretty much the story. We got hit on our bomb run over Hamburg. We limped back to Holland hoping to make it back over the channel to Britain, but our engines gave out. We had to bail out. I'm all right, as you can see, but my ankle's injured."

"I can see that."

"Have you heard anything? There were nine men in our crew. I wonder if the others are safe."

"Don't know nothing about that. Live here alone. My wife died several years ago. Don't have no radio. Only go into town every few months. But, Yank, I'd like to help you. We hate those rotten Nazis worse than anything. They take any of my crops they want, even took one of my cows. I can't sell anything. Steal everything that I don't eat."

"I'm sorry to hear that."

"Here, let me take a look at that foot. I guess it's your ankle."

Bill pulled up his pant leg and took off his boot to reveal the swollen and bloody ankle.

"You sure got a problem. We better soak it in hot water. Come over here by the stove and put your foot up on this chair. I'll heat some water."

He threw some wood on the fire in the cook stove and put on the kettle that he had filled with water from the pump in the sink. When the water boiled he poured it into an old pan, added some cold water to cool it a bit, and sat it on the floor in front of Bill's chair.

"Put your foot in here. This should relieve the pain a little."

Bill stuck his foot in the hot water. It did feel good, soothing the pain somewhat. "Are you sure this will help? At home we ice an injury like this."

"It'll help you."

After soaking it for a while, he gingerly put his foot on the ice cold stone floor to see if he could put his weight on it. It was obvious that he couldn't walk very far on that painful limb. His ankle was swollen and red. It looked like it was infected. As he sat back in the chair and put his foot up again, he wondered how long he could stay there and be cared for by the old man, who probably had trouble providing for himself.

"I'm afraid I won't be able to walk any distance until the swelling goes down."

"I can see that. You can stay here for a spell. Maybe I can figure something out."

Jan placed a beat-up ottoman under his foot. Getting his foot up relieved some of the pain. As he sat there watching him prepare a simple meal, Bill speculated on his situation. It was clear his circumstances were not as safe as they at first appeared. His host was elderly, bent over, probably with arthritis, and obviously having difficulty taking care of himself. Overcome with a wave of anxiety, Bill, once again, escaped the unpleasant reality of his situation by falling asleep in the chair.

Jan drank a mug of strong coffee with some homemade dark bread and went out into the sunshine, picked up his hoe in the shed, and cheerfully started to cultivate his vegetables. He had to figure out what to do with the airman, but, as he usually did, he put his thoughts aside, figuring a good idea would occur to him. In the meantime he'd get some of his necessary chores done. He knew he didn't have enough food to feed two men very long. He had to think of something. He recalled what his minister had always said, "God will provide." Being a practical man, he always figured God might need a little bit of help.

Over the next several days Bill's problem got worse. The redness and swelling spread up his leg. It was obviously infected. The flesh gave off a putrid smell. It was clear his minor injury was now becoming serious. The grizzled farmer took care of his every need, seeing that he had enough to eat and drink, and helping, in his way, to relieve his suffering. The soaking in hot water had helped some, but it had not stopped the spread of the inflammation. He had to get some antibiotics, and soon. How was the problem?

One morning, after a fitful night's sleep, he decided to broach the subject with the old man. "Jan, I hate to tell you this. But I've just got to get to a doctor. They have this medicine; it's called an antibiotic that cures an infection like this."

"You know, Lieutenant, I've been thinking. I know you're right. I can see what's going on. We'll have to risk it. We might be able to make it into town at night. There's a doc there I know. A kindly soul. Hates the Krauts like I do."

For the first time since he arrived, Bill managed a weak smile. "You know I can't put my weight on this foot. I can't walk very well."

"The truth is you can't walk at all. I'm strong like an ox. I can carry you. I've got an old truck in the barn. As soon as we get a dark night without a moon or stars we'll give it a try."

"I can't tell you how much I appreciate what you're doing."

Several days passed. Bill suffered with the throbbing pain. It was getting worse. One dark night after dinner of hearty potato soup, coarse brown bread and milk, Jan announced. "This's it, Lieutenant, we'll go tonight. You're only getting worse. And it's a black night. No one can spot us on a night like this."

"I was hoping you'd say that. I'm ready."

He knew his time was running out. He'd have to get to a doctor or risk losing his leg. It might already be too late for the drugs to work.

Jan came up with some worn overalls and a wool sweater and helped him change. He burned Bill's flight suit in the cook stove, for fear of an inspection by the Germans. If he was caught shielding the American boy they'd shoot him for sure.

CHAPTER VII

"Here, put your hands around my neck, hold on tight."

Jan's farmhouse

Jan knelt down and hoisted the one-hundered-and-sixty pound lieutenant, who hung on with all his might. Shuffling to the door he rested his load against the wall and swung the barn door open. Bill could just make out an ancient pickup truck in the darkness. Jan picked him up again, but getting him up into the cab proved to be a daunting challenge. First, he sat him on the running board, then climbed up into the cab and pulled him up into the cab. Bill was suffering excruciating pain and passed out.

Jan cranked the starter over and over. Just when he was about to give up the engine caught. Backing out into the darkness, he picked up the rutted dirt lane to the gravel road into town. As they bumped and jostled along Bill came to. He could scarcely make out the road. He was amazed at the old man's ability to stay on the route. With the pain he dozed off again only to awaken when they slowed down coming into town. He saw a row of small stone houses. This had to be the town he'd heard about.

Jan inched the truck up the street and turned into an alley behind the largest house Bill had seen.

He cut the engine. "Bill, you stay here. Keep quiet. This here's the doctor's house. I'll see if I can wake him."

Sliding down to the ground he walked up a garden path to the back door hidden from the street. Cautiously, he knocked on the door. There wasn't a sign of anyone awake. Then he thought of a better idea. He moved over under the doctor's bedroom, gathered up a handful of mud, formed it into a ball and tossed it at the window. Nothing happened. After several efforts he heard the window open and the irate doctor stuck his tousled head out and looked around.

He called out, "What's going on down there? Whose there?"

"Doctor, Doctor. It's your friend, Jan, Jan Cortsandt."

Obviously irritated, "What are you doing there? It's the middle of the night."

"Please, Doc. Open the door. I've got a sick man on my hands. Needs help."

Come back tomorrow in office hours. Can't you see I'm sleeping. You'll wake my wife."

"Can't do that. He's a Yank. Bailed out over Holland. Injured his ankle when he landed. It's badly infected. He's gonna die."

"Why didn't you say that in the first place? I'll be right down."

The rotund doctor slipped on his well worn slippers, hurried down the stairs and without turning on a light opened the door to confront the farmer.

"Where is he, can't see a thing?"

Jan pointed up into the cab where he could just make out a man slouched in the seat.

"Can he walk?"

"No, he can't. He's in bad shape."

Between the two of them they just managed to extricate Bill from the cab and carry him into the kitchen and the waiting room, where they stretched him out on an examination table.

The doctor asked in broken English, "Which leg is it?"

"My left one sir." Bill gasped.

He rolled up his bloody pant leg exposing the swollen and darkened leg and ankle. The rancid smell was unmistakable.

"I'm afraid young man; it's pretty bad, badly infected."

He took a thermometer out of a cabinet, shook it down and inserted it under Bill's tongue. He wasn't surprised when it read 104 degrees.

"You've got a dangerous fever. How do you feel?"

"To tell the truth, lousy. I hurt it when I hit the ground. Had to walk several days before I found his farm. He took good care of me, soaked it, but it got steadily worse."

"You're lucky he got you here. Known Jan for years. He used to swap meat and fresh vegetables when he couldn't afford to pay me. Roll up your sleeve. I'll give you a shot of penicillin. My name's DeVries, Hendrik Devries. What's yours?"

"Bill, Bill Richter. Lieutenant Bill Richter, United States Air Force."

The doctor rummaged through a drawer where he found a hypodermic needle, then took a bottle of penicillin out of an ice box, and carefully withdrew the prescribed amount.

"This might hurt a bit." He gently injected the antibiotic into his arm. "Now, lay back. I'll cover you up. We won't move you tonight." He covered Bill up with an embroidered throw his wife had made.

"One more thing. He said, to the half asleep patient, "You'll be all right here tonight, but first thing tomorrow, before my patients come in, we'll move you upstairs.

Jan had watched all of this, remaining silent out of respect for the doctor and his patient, then followed him into the kitchen. Doctor DeVries said, "Now, Jan, be very careful getting out of town. It's so quiet around here that anything unusual could be cause for alarm. You know, everybody knows everybody else's business." He clapped him on the back, "You did the right thing bringing him here. Be careful."

"Just hope he makes it."

"I do too. It's a powerful drug, but it's an advanced infection."

Jan climbed up into the cab, started the engine and cautiously crept through the darkened streets back to the comparative safety of his farm. He was proud of himself, having done something for the young American aviator and the cause, against the dreaded occupiers of his country.

Early the next morning the doctor came down stairs before the patients started coming. "Lieutenant, wake up. I've got to get you out of here right away. There's a patient coming in at eight."

Bill muttered, "I understand. Where you gonna put me?"

"I'll put you upstairs for now. You were in such bad shape I left you down here last night. You were out on your feet. How do you feel this morning?"

"I'll live."

"You young guys never want to admit you're sick. We're going to take you upstairs."

"They look pretty steep."

"We'll get you up there all right. I've got this big handyman. He could lift a house."

"Can you trust him? What about the Nazis?"

"Don't worry about that. He's been hassled by them before, hates them."

Just then a short muscular young Dutchman came into the room. "Mornin sir. Sorry ahm late. Guess I overslept. This here the Yank?"

"It is. I've told you before about being late. You take one side, and I'll take the other. We'll carry him upstairs."

"Sorry sir."

"Lift him up. Be careful. He's got a diseased leg."

They struggled up the stairs. It proved much more difficult than Hendrik had thought. They took him back to the spare bedroom and laid him out on the bed. Hendrik was out of breath, "Now Lieutenant, I'll leave you here until tonight. My wife, Johanna, will be up with a tray later. I've got to get to work. We'll be back after dark to move you."

He hurried downstairs thankful to be back in his regular routine. So far they had gotten away with it.

After a bit a good-looking young brunette came in bearing a breakfast tray. Smiling warmly, she looked over the young airman she'd heard about. In a soothing voice, she said, "Here Lieutenant, I've prepared a full breakfast for you. I'm the doctor's wife.

Are you hungry?" She spoke in broken English just like her husband.

He realized he hadn't eaten for quite a time, "Sure am Ma'am. I'm Bill, Bill Richter." He extended his hand.

"Mine's Johanna, Johanna DeVries."

He was ravenous. He hadn't had a square meal since he took off in England. It looked like a feast. Two hard boiled eggs, three slices of bacon, toast and jam and a mug of steaming coffee.

Ignoring the young beauty, he gulped it down. He felt good for awhile but the pain quickly returned.

She could see the suffering on his face, "Don't worry. You'll be better soon. Here's a little bell. Ring it if you need something." She swished out of the room to get back to work with her husband.

He was already treating a local tradesman. He turned to her, "How's he doing? Any better?"

"In a lot of pain. Ate well though. As the Americans say, he's a macho guy, won't admit he's hurting. Good looking too."

"I thought you'd say that. Let's get to work."

Later Johanna brought lunch up to Bill. They scarcely talked, but he did thank her profusely for the meal. He hurt so much he didn't feel like talking, even to her.

After dinner DeVries came up to give Bill his shot. "We'll move you out later tonight. I've made arrangements with our domonei to take you in. We think it should be safe there. You know, he's our minister in the

Dutch Reformed Church. They've never searched the rectory, but getting you there is the dangerous part.

"I understand. I know all the risks you're taking. I appreciate it."

"Don't give it a thought. You couldn't imagine what our lives are like now. People are in constant fear. Sometime we can talk about it. How'd you like Johanna's cooking?"

"Couldn't be better."

Bill had dinner that night served by the pretty young wife. Fortunately, it turned out to be a dark night. He waited impatiently for the move certain he'd be safer then.

When the door flew open DeVries and his man came in. "Well, lad are you ready to go?"

"Ready as I'll ever be."

"How's the ankle?"

"Still there. Maybe a little better."

They helped him out of bed and down the stairs, out the back door and into the back seat of the doctor's Volvo. The handyman crawled in next to Bill. "Suh, if you'd be so kind? Keep yer head down."

Bill hunched down, unable to see outside, as they bumped along the rutted street. He sat up when they pulled into a driveway and saw that they were met by a tall distinguished looking man in clerical garb. He walked up to the car and said to Hendrik, "So this is your charge? You amaze me, Doctor. How did you get involved in this? I didn't think you were in the resistance."

"I'm not. It just happened; he has a bad infection in his leg. I'm caring for him."

"Wouldn't he be better off at your home where you have all the equipment?"

"That's out of the question. He's an American aviator who had to bail out over the Zuider Zee. Was injured when he hit the ground. Somehow, he managed to make it to Cortstandt's farm. Jan protected him, brought him into me when he was ill. The Germans are after him, we know that. If he's picked up in civilian clothes he'd probably be executed as a spy. We've heard some gruesome stories of how they're treating prisoners-of-war."

"I didn't know all that. He should be safe here. I don't think they'll come in here. At least I don't think they will."

Bill had carefully listened to all of this. He wondered what kind of a man this cleric might be. "Don't worry about me, Rector. With a few more shots I'll be ready to go."

Hendrik interjected, “Sorry to say, that’s ridiculous. It’ll take weeks, maybe months, for the antibiotic to work. Then you’ll have to rehab your leg. You’re just lucky Jan brought you in when he did. I’ve got to get going, you know, work on my records. Just remember, without the Americans this war would never be won. We owe them a lot. By the way, Bill, Johanna will bring your dinners over after dark.”

The domonei said, “I guess you realize, Doctor, I’m getting older and my wife isn’t too well. Before the war I was a pacifist, but after I saw what the Nazis were doing in this country I changed my mind. Jesus said we should love one another and not kill, but come what may we’ve got to get them out of Holland.”

“Amen to that. Goodbye, Lieutenant, you’ll be safe here. He’s a good man. You can trust him.”

“I can see that. Thanks for all your help.”

As the days passed Bill grew stronger, with the shots, and the attentions of Johanna. They seemed to hit it off, had some interesting conversations about Holland, the Dutch, America and the Americans. The good looking young American was fascinating to her after the somber life she and her husband had been living since the war. It seemed like the people of Metternich had more complaints since the Nazis had showed up. Hendrik thought it was all the stress they were under and the lack of a healthy diet. It was difficult to carry on under these circumstances.

CHAPTER VIII

"He was sure he'd succeed in time."

Metternich, Holland

Time passed slowly in the rectory. Bill gradually gained strength, starting to feel like his old self again. The penicillin had performed its miraculous function. The swelling went down and the ankle was healing. The worst pain was past, but he had to work hard to rebuild his muscles so that he could walk again. The good doctor had given him a set of exercises and he worked diligently at these. At first he hobbled around the room, and later around the house when it was safe. He had to remain secluded in the room when anybody called on the domenei. The highlight of the day was when the doctor's voluptuous young wife came up with his dinner. She fascinated him. How could such a gorgeous young thing be married to the much older doctor?

It was obvious she enjoyed coming to see him that she didn't just come out of a sense of duty. One sunny day she showed up looking unusually vivacious, decked out in a rather revealing blouse and tight fitting skirt. Why had she bothered to dress so attractively?

"Bill, I've brought you something special for dinner. You'll like this." She swept a cloth off the tray to reveal a pork chop with mashed potatoes and gravy.

"I don't know how you do it. With the food shortages and all. Aren't the shortages getting worse?"

She smiled charmingly, "It's like this. Money's so short many of the farmers pay us with food. One of them just butchered a pig and shared the meat with us. We're better fed than anybody in town. It is sort of embarrassing. I've been giving some to the rector's wife. He doesn't get paid that much. Church contributions are way off."

"I've been wondering, Johanna, do you hear anything about the outside world? You know the rest of the country?"

"Not too much."

"I haven't heard a word about the rest of the crew. I do know the captain got down. I saw his parachute. I haven't seen him since."

"Sorry to say, I haven't. Haven't heard a thing. We did hear the war's going better. The Allies are preparing to invade France." She sighed, "I still believe we'll win."

"I'm sure we will. If you do hear any thing will you let me know?"

"I certainly will. This horrible war can't go on forever. How was your dinner?"

"You can see I ate every morsel. It was great, just great."

As she bent over to retrieve the tray, Bill was tempted by the curve of her ample breasts, revealed seductively in her low cut blouse. He took her tiny hand in his and attempted a kiss. She blushed and pulled away. "Now, now, Lieutenant, none of that. I'm a married woman."

"I know. I'm sorry. I'll be a good boy. Don't tell the doctor."

"Of course not. I'm not a child." She rushed out of the room.

He called out, "Will I see you tomorrow?"

"You will." She was flattered by his attentions. She had to be careful to control herself, as the truth was she found him terribly attractive. He had trouble sleeping that night. He knew she welcomed his interest even though she protested. It was obvious from her body language. He'd always had his way with girls. There was something about him they couldn't resist. But some of the most desirable, like Johanna, played hard to get. He'd bide his time.

She was sort of formal the next week, obviously nervous, afraid of what he might do next. It was amazing though. She was better dressed, with her hair carefully brushed and her pretty white blouse. But she was careful not to get too close. With little else to think about he, was obsessed with the girl. He knew he should leave her alone, but it was a challenge. Making out would be such fun.

She loved to ask questions about America. She had never traveled out of the country, but she had read a lot about the states. One evening, to his surprise, she pulled up a chair and sat down, still so he couldn't reach her.

"Bill, where do you come from in the states?"

"Indiana." He blurted out.

"Where's Indiana?"

Annoyed at this diversion, he snapped, "in the center of the country."

"I can't imagine a country can be so big."

"Well, it is. It's huge and beautiful. You'd never believe how varied the terrain is, what with the oceans, the plains and the mountains."

"What's Indiana like?'

"It's right in the middle of the country. It's a Midwestern state, you know, the heartland. It's pretty flat. Have you ever heard of Indianapolis?"

"Indian what? No, I haven't."

Bill chuckled, "Indianapolis. It's the largest city in Indiana. Home of the Indy 500."

"What in the world is that?"

"It's a famous car race. The biggest race in the world. They go over a hundred."

"Like the race at Monte Carlo?"

"I guess, sort of. People come from all over the world to see it. They have a big track and grandstands. Some of the best racing cars in the world."

"Bill, there's something I've been meaning to ask you. Are you married?"

"Nah, nothing like that. Just an eligible bachelor."

"I just wondered. I've got to get going. The doctor will be looking for me. See you tomorrow." Trying to conceal her pleasure, she hurried out of the room.

In subsequent days their conversation became more personal. One day he asked, "Johanna, would you answer a question for me? How'd you happen to marry an older man?"

Her first reaction was to say it's none of your business. But it was nice to have somebody to talk to. "That's a difficult question. I come from a poor family, good people, but we didn't have much. Doctors are so rich."

"You married for money?"

"Nothing of the kind. He was such a gentleman, so nice. He courted me with flowers and presents. His first wife had died. He was all alone. I felt sorry for him. My mother liked him too. He was so courteous and polite, not at all like the boys I had known."

"Were you in love with him?"

"I don't know what you mean by love. We don't have time for romantic love like you Americans. We're too poor for that. It was a good match. I thought I was so lucky. A man like that liking me. Treats me with respect, kindly, you know. He's never let on he married down."

"Well, that's nice. I can see why you married him. But true love, that's another thing."

"Piffle, who has time for that? We're too busy for that."

"Perhaps that's the reason. Let me tell you, it's the most wonderful thing in the world."

"I think you're just talking about sex. That's just a momentary pleasure, more like a duty."

"A duty? I can't believe you said that." With this he remained quiet. It would take a long time to convince her real what love and passion were all about.

CHAPTER IX

"His clever strategy wasn't working so far."

Metternich, Holland

As Bill grew stronger his obsession with Johanna overcame any moral reservations he might have had. He could hardly wait for her visits. Their pleasant but superficial relationship had morphed into an intensity they had not expected, driven by his sexual desires, his need for conquest and her efforts to control her urges. He wondered how he could overcome her inhibitions. She was obviously nervous around him, tempted but not ready to let go. She said no, but her body language said yes.

One evening after she left, it came to him. He'd flatter her and lead her on by pretending to be in love. He'd never really been in love with anyone, except perhaps his mother.

She struggled to keep their relationship on a friendly but proper basis. She owed so much to her husband. He supported her, treated her with respect and often catered to her childish whims. She thought she'd distract Bill by engaging in general discussions and not get too close to resist his temptations.

The next evening he said, "Johanna, you look ravishing, the prettiest thing I ever saw."

She blushed, "Now, now, none of that nonsense. I was just thinking. I want to ask you some more questions about America."

"What about America?"

"Have you ever been to New York?'

"No, I have not."

"I heard it's a beautiful city, with all its wealth and theatre."

"I suppose it is."

"I read they have great stage plays there, you know, theatre."

"They probably do."

"Have you ever been to a Broadway show?"

"I already told you I haven't been there."

"I'm sorry Bill, I forgot."

"I'm just a down-to-earth Midwesterner."

"What do you do there in Indiana?"

"I'm a pharmacist. I prepare prescriptions for sick people."

"Do you enjoy that work?"

"It's sort of boring, but pays well. What about you? Don't you ever want to travel? Have you ever been out of Holland?"

"That's out of the question. I have to help my husband. He can't afford a nurse. I've learned a lot working for him."

"I'll bet you have. Don't you ever dream of a more glamorous life, with travel and interesting people?"

She looked glum, "That's ridiculous. Sounds like something out of the movies. I'm just a simple person. I love this town. It's good here, even with our simple ways. Hendrik is a good man."

"I'm sure he is. But it doesn't sound too romantic. Would you think it was?"

The conversation was getting personal despite her good intentions. "Now, Bill, you've got to stop talking to me like this. It's nonsense anyway. What you Americans mean by love I'll never understand. I have it good. We believe in hard work and responsibility. Not all this frivolous tripe you're talking about."

His clever strategy wasn't working so far. But he'd never been one to give up easily. He knew she found him attractive. Deep down she had to dream of a better life. How could a pretty young thing like Johanna be happy married to a middle-aged overweight man who worked all the time?"

Hendrik had begun to notice that she seemed preoccupied, not her normal self. She'd always been so meticulous in her work, anticipating his every move. Now he had to remind her of the next step and when he needed medicine or instruments. But she was still good with patients. They all seemed to like her. Sometimes he thought they liked her better than him. He had also noticed she was dressing better and more careful with her hair and makeup.

One morning at breakfast, he asked, "Dear, I wonder what's happening? You seem to be having trouble concentrating on your work. Is it something I've done? Are you tired?"

Her face reddened, "No, nothing like that. It's nothing you've done. We do seem to have more patients now. Why is that?"

"It's hard to say. It is sort of a difficult occupation. Maybe the people are under more stress now with the Germans and all. They don't have enough food. It's nothing we can do anything about. We do have it good compared to most people."

"I know you're right about that, dear. To tell the truth I think you're working too hard."

She didn't want to tell him she felt neglected. That would be silly. They hardly ever had any time alone together and he did seem grumpy at times and difficult to talk to.

"That's just the way it is. I've got my responsibilities. They depend on me. These are difficult times but it will pass. Maybe it won't be long now. We have a busy day. We'd better get at it."

Hendrik seemed even more preoccupied after their conversation. They seemed to see more patients than ever. Many of their complaints seemed psychological to her. After their evening meal and her visit with Bill, Hendrik quietly read his paper and fell into bed thoroughly exhausted without even a kiss and certainly not sex. It was a grueling regimen.

Her evening visits with the young American became the highlight of her day. She looked forward to his attentions as long as they remained within proper bounds. There was nothing wrong with it. They were just friends.

Bill's spirits rose. He sensed that she liked him and the war news was encouraging. She was obviously pleased to see him but careful not to get close. He wanted to grab her and force himself on her, but even he knew that was wrong. Making love to her obsessed his thoughts. He'd never felt this strongly about any other girl.

Johanna realized she wasn't worldly wise. She had been brought up in a poor but strict family in Metternich. But she knew what men always wanted. She'd gone out with some before she married. She believed that American men were just like the Dutch, preoccupied with sex. She had strong urges just like any other woman her age. But she knew she had responsibilities as a wife and that she owed Hendrik a lot. It was wonderful to have a nice young friend to talk to, but he was just a friend, nothing more, nothing less.

CHAPTER X

"I'll pretend you never said such a thing."

Metternich, Holland

Bill decided he'd make another move on her. She was such a knock out, the sexiest thing he'd ever seen. When she came in one night he decided now was the time, "Johanna, I've got something important to say to you."

She giggled, "What is it, for goodness sake?"

"It's just that, now don't laugh. I'm in love with you."

She turned crimson, "In love, in love, how could that be? You hardly know me." She laughed nervously.

"Don't make fun of me. I'm serious. Never been so serious in my life. I love you; you're so beautiful and kind."

"Don't say things like that. I'll pretend you never said that. I'm a married woman."

"I can't forget it. Come over here, Johanna."

Despite her resolutions she moved over to his side. She knew it was wrong, but she couldn't help herself.

He put his arms around her and gave her a long passionate kiss. She kissed him back. He pulled her down into his lap and kissed her again and again. They were like young lovers. He started to gently massage her heaving breast. She gasped, "Stop that. Please don't."

He ignored her entreaties, putting his hand up under her skirt and touching her pussy through her underpants. She moaned, helpless to stop him. Her resolve was gone. It was never like this with her husband. He massaged her tenderly. She was transfixed by the exhilaration of the moment.

He picked her up and carried her to the bed and ripped off her clothes. They made impassioned love, until fully sated, they were exhausted.

Bill kissed her once more, "Now, you know how much I really love you."

Johanna struggled up from the bed, quickly dressed, rearranged her rumpled clothes and combed her hair. When she looked in a mirror she looked a fright. She had to wash and make herself up before Hendrik saw her. She had to be careful. He was so perceptive. He'd know something was wrong.

She gave Bill a searching look, "Now, Lieutenant, I want you to know. This can never happen again. I can't go on like this. I should have never let myself go."

Bill smiled benevolently, "You're probably right. I'm sorry if it upset you, but I do love you."

She blushed, "Don't say that again. It's an impossible situation."

"All right, my dear, I'll try to be good."

He knew they were committed lovers, regardless of what she said. His affairs only ended when he was tired of the girl. That seemed unlikely in this case.

She drove back home, quietly slipped into the house, and went to the lavatory to wash and make herself up. When she entered the sitting room Hendrik looked up from his paper and asked, "Where have you been. You've been gone so long. Is everything all right?"

"He's doing well. He just likes to talk. He's curious how we live here. Perhaps he finds Holland interesting."

"Oh, that's it." He buried his face in the paper again.

Bill's secret prediction proved true. Almost every evening after his dinner, or sometimes even before, they made love in the bedroom. It was like a whole new world for her. She had never experienced anything like this. She was hopelessly and desperately in love. It was never like this with Hendrik. They rarely had sex, and even then, it was quick and unemotional. She almost never had a climax. She viewed it as her duty as a wife, not something necessarily to be enjoyed. She did want very much to have a child and this was a necessary preliminary.

This new relationship with the good looking young American was other worldly. He flattered, kissed and caressed her. They made love in all sorts of new and interesting ways. She knew in the back of her mind that he would be going home some day, but she couldn't help herself. It was beyond reason; a level of passion she had never known existed.

Hendrik noticed a difference in her. She seemed strangely preoccupied, unable to concentrate. She'd always been so efficient, now she was clumsy. One morning at breakfast he got up his nerve and confronted her, "My dear, I've been meaning to ask you. You don't seem like yourself. Aren't you well? Is something wrong?"

She blurted, "No, nothing! Nothing at all!"

"What is it then?"

"I'm just tired. We've been working so hard. It's the war and all. It seems to be getting to me."

"I'm sorry dear. You're so young. I guess the strain is getting to all of us. Maybe I've been pushing too hard. I'll try to ease up.

"Maybe that will help." She went over and gave him a kiss on the cheek and hurried to the kitchen to avoid any more questions.

He did let up for a few days, but soon they were right back to the frenetic pace. She was obviously having trouble keeping up, even dropping things with patients present. He'd have to get to the bottom of this. Perhaps she just didn't want to talk about her problems. She had always been reluctant to discuss her private thoughts with him. He'd have to think it over but he never seemed to have time to think about her with all the work and the difficulties of the occupation.

CHAPTER XI

"This was a worrisome complication."

Metternich, Holland: 1944

The affair came to dominate her thoughts. For the first time in her life she was carried away in love with a man. Being a practical girl she knew her marriage to the doctor was the best thing for her. They had a comfortable life together. She enjoyed helping people in the clinic. It made her feel needed. But then there was Bill, so young and glamorous. He made her feel alive. She knew her mother would never approve of what she had done, or even understand why she did it. Try as she might, she couldn't stop. Caught up in the moment, she was unable to face the reality of her marriage.

Hendrik was working harder than ever. But he was increasingly suspicious of what was going on. He had tried to lessen the pressure on her, but it did not help; she continued to be preoccupied and forgetful. One night in bed he resolved to get to the bottom of things. He couldn't consider eavesdropping for he was a professional man. It would be beneath his dignity. Perhaps he was just getting paranoid, preoccupied with suspicious thoughts. It was getting to him. He had difficulty concentrating. Something had to be done.

The very next day over coffee at the breakfast table he mustered up his courage. "Johanna, as I said before, you don't seem yourself. You've been having difficulty keeping up. What's the problem? What's going on?"

She flushed, aghast at the direct question, so unlike him, "It's nothing dear, nothing at all. I'm just tired."

He persevered in a stern voice, "You said that before. I can't accept that answer. You don't look tired when you come back from the parsonage."

"I just enjoy talking to the Lieutenant. I like to hear about America."

"I hope you haven't become involved with him."

"Involved? How could I be involved? Nothing of the sort."

She had always prided herself on being honest with him, but she couldn't tell the truth. She didn't want to hurt him.

He gave her a severe stare, "We have to get to work. We've got a heavy schedule today."

She hung her head and followed meekly along to the clinic and another long hard day.

He was not satisfied with her answers but he had to figure out how to get the truth. The long days wore on with little time to think about Johanna and her strange behavior.

His suspicions came to the fore one evening after she came back from her nightly visit. She had been crying. Her darling little face was flushed. She looked shaken.

He looked up from his paper, "What's wrong? You look a fright. Why have you been crying?"

Tears streamed down uncontrollably, "Oh, Hendrik. I've got to tell the truth. I love him."

He cried out outraged, "You love him?"

"I can't help myself. It's just that I'm so young and all. I didn't want this to happen. I know I owe you so much. You've been a good husband."

His face writhed with pain, "How could you do this to me? Haven't I been good to you?"

"You always have. Maybe I married too young. I never wanted this."

He shouted in her face, "This has to stop! You'll never see him again. Do you understand? I'll have our girl, Miriam, take him his meals. You're not to ever see him again. Is that clear?"

Overcome by tears, she rushed up the stairs, where she fell on the bed, until exhausted, she fell asleep.

For days she moped around the house, reluctantly obeying his orders. She looked a sight. She stopped making herself up or combing her hair and seldom got out of her housecoat. Hardly a word passed between them. She was devastated not being able to see Bill or even talk with him.

Hendrik was even more suspicious of what had been going on. Had it been a childish infatuation or what? If they had been physically intimate it was all over between them. He had to find out. Finally, he decided. He'd confront the son-of-a-bitch. He had years of experience interviewing. He knew how to get things out of people.

The next evening after another day's hard work he drove his Volvo over to the parsonage. The domonei was amazed to see him at that hour. He'd never been back since Bill's leg healed.

"Why, Doctor, what a surprise. What brings you out at this hour?"

Hendrik looked grim, "It's just that I've been terribly busy. I wanted to see how the patient was doing."

"Oh, that's it. I won't detain you then. It is good to see you. One of these days, maybe we could get together and discuss the church finances."

"I'd be glad to do that, but not now."

"I'll look forward to that. You know where his room is, upstairs in the back."

Hendrik bolted up the stairs and charged through the door without knocking, confronting Bill reading in the armchair.

Bill looked up, astonished to see him, "Why, Doctor, what brings you out on a night like this?"

"Don't give me that. You know very well why I'm here."

"If you think I do, you're ahead of me. Here, take the easy chair."

Hendrik gave him a threatening look, "Listen here, young man. My wife's beside herself, moping around the house, can't stop crying."

"I'm sorry to hear that. What's that got to do with me?"

"It's got everything to do with you. She claims she's in love with you. Is that true? I think you took advantage of her."

"I never took advantage of her. She threw herself at me. She was starved for affection. You just work all the time and ignore her."

Hendrik stiffened, overcome with hostility, "You mean to tell me you've had sex with my wife. You admit it. I can't believe how evil you are. After all I've done for you. You've ruined our marriage for your selfish enjoyment."

Bill feigned indignation, "I felt sorry for her. The poor thing needed affection. She never got it from you."

"What do you know about that?"

"She told me."

Hendrik could hardly restrain himself. He felt like punching him in the mouth. He yelled, "I'll get you for this! You'll be sorry." He wheeled around, bolted out the door and slammed it behind him.

When he got back home Johanna had already gone to bed. Over breakfast the following morning, he announced, "Last night, I went to see Bill Richter."

"What'd you do that for?"

"I wanted to find out the truth."

"I already told you what happened."

"It seems you didn't tell the whole story. He admitted you had been lovers. Is that true?"

She whispered, barely able to get the words out, "It will never happen again."

His face was livid, "That's the end of our marriage. Get out, you whore. We're through!" He started out the door.

"Hendrik." She called out pathetically. "I love you. Haven't I been a good wife? I'll be faithful. It'll never happen again. I promise." Tears streamed down her face.

"It's too late now, no apologies. Pack up and get out. I never want to see you again."

"Where will I go? Mother is poor. What'll I do?"

"You should have thought of that. Get out of my sight. I can't stand looking at you."

Johanna felt as if her life was falling apart. She struggled up the long stairs and started packing, but unable to concentrate, threw herself on the bed in a shroud of tears.

Hendrik hurried back to his office, eager to bury himself in his work and put her out of his mind. He never did understand women. But, he had loved her. This was the end of a good marriage that had been the joy of his life.

With Johanna gone he was miserable. His hostility toward the American fed on itself. He had to get even. He'd never been a violent man, but he'd get him, one way or another. He thought and thought what to do. Finally, he decided. He'd turn him over to the Nazis who would regard him as a spy, dressed in civilian clothes. He had to be very careful to avoid implicating himself or the domonei. It had to be a foolproof plan. If the townspeople found out he'd be ruined. They'd never forgive consorting with the enemy. He had difficulty sleeping, neglected his personal appearance and had difficulty doing justice to his work. For days on end he didn't shave and wore wrinkled and spotty clothes. Without Johanna's help he had difficulty keeping up.

One morning, their maid, ran into him in the hallway.

"Doctor, I've got somthin I've gotta tell you. With the missus gone you don't look yourself. Never saw you like this. What'll your patients think? Ah hope you'll forgive me for saying this."

He snapped, "What's it matter to you? It's none of your business."

"Yer right sir. Thought I might help."

He felt guilty, treating her so shabbily. "Sorry I said that. You could lay out some clean clothes for me."

It was difficult to concentrate on his patient's problems plotting his revenge. He'd have to get him out of the parsonage to a neutral site, where they'd believe he'd been hiding. It would be easy getting him out of there at night but the best site was another matter.

Miriam laid out some clean pressed clothes but she couldn't see much improvement in his appearance. He looked sloppy with his hair uncombed and his tie askew. She'd done all she could, but she needed her job there. She decided to just go about her duties and try to ignore his strange behavior. It was probably due to his wife leaving. She never did understand what had happened between them.

One dark stormy night Hendrik drove, with his handyman, across town to the parsonage. Climbing the stairs two steps at a time, he charged in unannounced. He found the lieutenant lounging in an easy chair, reading a book and smoking a cigarette. Looking contented, he grinned, "Why, Doctor, this is a surprise. What do I owe the honor of this visit?"

He bellowed, "Get up out of there! You're moving. I've a perfect spot for you. The Nazis are all over. It's not safe here. You can hide out in the woods."

"Why all this concern? It isn't any worse than it was, is it?" Bill was suspicious. He was happy there with the good food and kindly cleric. "What are you up to? I like it here. I'm not going."

"It doesn't matter what you think. You're going. Get your things together."

Bill settled back in the chair ignoring the order.

Hendrik stepped out into the hall and signaled the handyman to come in. The two of them advanced on Bill, "Get up or we'll take you any way necessary."

He jumped up to resist but was quickly restrained by the muscular handyman by a blow to the head. They dragged him out the door and down the stairs and shoved him into the back seat of the car. Hendrik drove slowly through the sleeping town out into the country to deep woods, where he picked up a rutted trail deeper into the forest. They bumped along about a half hour until he pulled up to a shack that had been years ago shelter for woodsmen. He had stumbled on it one time hunting.

They led him into the building and sat him down on a crude wooden bench. Hendrik would never forget the look on Bill's face when he realized what they had done to him. He carefully locked the door with a rusty padlock and drove back home. He thanked his man, gave him a generous tip and swore him to secrecy.

When he was alone he dialed the number of the German headquarters in Metternich. A trooper answered in an angry voice. "Wot you want?"

"This is Doctor DeVries. Get your officer in charge. I've captured a spy."

"Wots this?" The sergeant yelled. "It's the middle of the night. He's sleeping, can't be disturbed. Never heard of you. Call tomorrow." He was furious being awakened from his nap.

For Hendrik, this was a worrisome complication. How long would Bill be safe out there? But there wasn't anything else he could do until morning. He'd have to call back during office hours and see if he could reach somebody in charge.

He didn't sleep well that night, tossed and turned, mulling over the events of the day. He still couldn't believe that rotten American had seduced his wife, ruined his marriage, and turned his life upside down. Maybe if he couldn't get the authorities to go out there he'd starve to death. It would serve him right.

He struggled out of bed at six, threw on his clothes and fixed himself a pot of strong coffee. Right at nine he dialed the number. The same stupid trooper answered. "Good morning, Sergeant. This is Doctor De Vries. Is your officer in charge there? Remember, I called last night."

"Yes sir, I told him wot you said. He'll talk to you."

"I'll be right over."

He put on his heavy wool sweater and cap and walked the few blocks to the Gestapo office. It was a cold and windy day. With the exhilaration the cold air felt good. It served to sharpen his mind. He enjoyed realizing that Bill was suffering from the cold and lack of food. For the first time since his breakup with Johanna he felt good, as he hummed a Dutch tune.

When he arrived at the huge stone building, a mansion commandeered by the Nazis, formerly the property of a wealthy townsman, he rapped on the huge door. The sergeant stuck his head out, greeted Hendrik rudely, patted him down and ordered him into a straight back chair. "Sit there." He reluctantly obeyed not used to being ordered around.

Hendrik waited impatiently as visitors came and went. At long last, near noon, the sergeant announced in halting Dutch, "Herr Doctor, he'll see you now. Follow me."

Hendrik followed along and was escorted into a cavernous office where a square-jawed officer, with a butch cut and ugly scar on his face, presided behind an immense desk elevated to keep him in a superior position. For Hendrik he personified the arrogant Nazi reveling in his authority over the Dutch.

The sergeant snapped to and saluted, "Heil Hitler. This here's Doctor De Vries, Commandant."

Hendrik extended his hand, but was ignored.

The commandant glared at Hendrik contemptuously, "What's this fairy tale about a spy?"

"Good morning sir. How are you?"

"Get on with it. None of that ridiculous Dutch talk. Wot do you want? You Dutch always want something."

Hendrik's face reddened, "I don't want anything." He swallowed nervously, "I want to help you. I found this American spy hiding in the woods."

The commandant, suddenly interested, leaned forward, "You've found an American in the woods. What were you doing there? It's not allowed."

"I'm a hunter. I was hunting. I locked him in a shack until you could apprehend him."

"Why didn't you tell Hans about this?"

"I told him last night but he wouldn't listen. I told him I had important information."

"We get people saying that every day." He jumped up and ordered, "Hans, get a squad. There's an American spy in the woods."

Hans clicked his heels, saluted and rushed out to call out the squad.

Four young German soldiers tumbled out of the nearby guardhouse and assembled on the cobbled street, waiting for Hans to pull up the lorry. They quickly crowded in back, guns at the ready. The commandant and the doctor sat up in front with Hans, where Hendrik pointed the way out of town and onto the rutted path in the deep woods.

When they pulled up in front of the wretched shack, the German officer sneered. "So, this is it? It doesn't look strong enough to hold anyone."

"Yes sir. This is it. Let's see if he's still here."

"Bear in mind. If you're not telling the truth what will happen to you."

"Don't worry. I'm telling the truth." Secretly, he prayed that Bill was still there.

The officer motioned the squad to surround the building. When they were in position, he stode up to the door and gave it a shake. It wouldn't budge. "Get over here and unlock this thing."

Hendrik hurried to obey, pleased that it was still securely locked. He dug the key out of his pants and struggled to unlock the rusty padlock. Finally, it gave way. He shoved the door open and was pleased to find Bill Richter sitting on the bunk looking dazed and bewildered. The squad charged in and surrounded the victim.

Bill was aghast. He surveyed the unlikely scene and said hesitantly, "What's going on sir? I'm an officer in the United States Air Force. I deserve to be treated as a prisoner of war under the Geneva Convention."

The commandant grabbed him by the shoulder, and yelled in his face, "You don't have any rights. You're a spy. You're under arrest as a spy."

He ordered the troopers, "Bind and gag him. Put him in the lorry."

They hurried to obey, roughly bound him, and manhandled him into the vehicle.

Not a word was said on the drive back through the woods to the headquarters. Hendrik knew his plan was working out. He was fortunate that Richter was still there. It had been a dangerous enterprise but it looked like he had pulled it off.

They marched Bill into the office. When they searched him they found his dog tags, unmistakable proof that he was an American officer in civilian clothes.

Under intense questioning and threats of violence, Bill revealed only his name, rank and serial number. They dragged him out and downstairs to a prison cell.

The commandant stood up and shook Hendrik's hand. "You've done good work, Herr Doctor. We'll deal with this filthy spy."

Hendrik grinned, "He'll get what he deserves?"

"Don't worry. We'll take good care of him."

"I'll be off then. Got to care for my patients." He walked briskly home whistling the same happy tune. He was thankful he'd achieved his objective.

He slept soundly that night. It was like closure. He'd reaped his vengeance and that was the end of it—but was it? He'd have to deal with his guilt over helping the enemy.

The next morning it dawned on him. He had exacted retribution but had committed an unpatriotic act. He'd have to live with that guilt for the rest of his life. In a moment of hatred, he'd been guilty of an unpatriotic act; his hatred had overcome his love of country.

CHAPTER XII

"How'd it be if I took care of the rabbit?"

June-December, 1944; Groot, Holland

The days and weeks passed slowly in Gretel's household. Bored with the routine and fearful only of the patrols, Jim idled away the time unable to do anything constructive. It was against his nature to sit around all the time. The only things to read were some old Dutch books and magazines. He resorted to playing mind games and reminiscing about his past life in the states. His family would assume he was dead. Maybe his girl friend would move on to more fertile fields. He was too young to dwell on the past, but what else was there to do? Preoccupied with food and the damned dog, he got up earlier and earlier to beat him to the rocker, which he seldom did.

His arms and legs were shrinking, but for some strange reason, his belly was getting bigger. One morning at breakfast, "Gretel, I can't understand what's happening. I'm losing weight in my arms and legs, which were probably too fat anyway, but my stomach is swollen. I had to let out several notches on my belt."

"I hate to tell you this Captain, but the reason is you're not getting enough to eat. I'm doing the best I can, but food is very scarce right now. It's the worst I've seen. We went through those supplies that Nels brought."

"I know you're doing your best. Don't think I don't appreciate it."

"I'm hoping he'll bring some more. We haven't had any vegetables in a long time."

Jim couldn't figure out how Jacob looked so trim and well fed. It was shameful to be preoccupied with petty complaints when he was in relative safety with Gretel and Nels.

One night he hit on a scheme to get back at that pesty dog. The next morning he got up early, quickly dressed and hurried down to the kitchen. He snuck up behind the sleeping dog and jerked the rocker out from under him. He grinned like a kid when the obnoxious animal somersaulted onto the stone floor. Grabbing the rocker before the dog had a chance to recover he luxirated in the comfortable chair, cozied up to the warmth of the cook stove.

When Jacob came in he studied the scene and grumbled, "What happened to my dog? Did you kick him?"

Jim reddened, "Why would I kick your dog?"

"Obviously, you don't like him."

"I like dogs. Can't you see that?"

Jacob gave him a dirty look, but for once was out of words.

In the long run the dog always won. He'd listen for Jim's footsteps and jump in the rocker before he got there and warn him off with snarling teeth. Jim knew he would have to come up with a better scheme and wait for the opportune moment. He was obsessed with the trivial, but determined to win the battle. He had always thought about big things, like American history, but here he was preoccupied with the stupid dog and getting the rocker.

When Gretel came in, she asked, "How'd you two like a nice drink of warm milk?

"Where'd you ever get that?" Jim asked.

"One of my neighbors has a goat out back. She's a generous soul. Gave us some milk."

For a brief spell the tension in the kitchen dissipated as they enjoyed their unexpected treat.

One evening after dinner, they heard the unmistakable sound of a lorry coming up the street. Gretel shouted, "Grab your things. They're checking houses."

Jim had neglected to have all his belongings in the kitchen. He dashed down the hallway to his bedroom, gathered up his few belongings, his shaving brush and razor, and raced back to pull up the seat and clamber down into the damp cold tunnel. He groped around but was unable to find the candle. It smelled musty. He was afraid he might sneeze with his allergy problem.

They heard furious pounding on the front door. Gretel moved slowly to the door and opened it a crack, where she was confronted by a burly red-faced sergeant, furious at the delay."

In a sweet voice, “Can I help you Sergeant?”

He glared and shouted, “Why didn’t you open immediately?” Not waiting for an answer he shoved past her into the room.

She called after him, “You never know who might be out at night.”

He rummaged through the house, slamming cupboards and doors, in a vain attempt to find evidence of someone in hiding. The two other younger troopers with him finished the search by checking the kitchen and the privy. Jim held his breath when one of them came over to the bench. He tried to lift the seat but it failed to budge. At long last Jim heard them slam the front door and the lorry moved up the street. Once more they had survived an inspection. Would they always be able to outsmart the Germans or would they eventually be found out?

The next day life in the safe house resumed its tedious routine. When Jacob went into town one day, Jim approached Gretel once more. “How’d it be if I helped you with the housework? All you do is work around here. I don’t have a thing to do. What’s Jacob do anyway?”

“Jacob scrounges around for firewood at night for the stove.”

“I forgot about that. Couldn’t you please give me some chores to do? I used to help Mom at home.”

I couldn’t have a man cleaning my house. That would never do. What if the neighbors found out? I’d never live it down.”

“You sound like Mom. She didn’t want a man messing around in her house. But there’s gotta be something I could do. I can’t stand just sitting around.”

“I’ll think about it.”

Gretel had a little brown and white rabbit in a cage out by the outhouse that she religiously fed and watered every day. One morning Jim had an idea. “How’d it be if I took care of that rabbit? That wouldn’t be housework.”

“You know, that would be nice. There isn’t much to it. I just feed and water it every day and occasionally clean out the cage.”

“That sounds great. I’ll start tomorrow. What do you feed it?”

“Just some left over potato peelings and grass and weeds from out back.”

“Be very careful out there. The stone wall will screen you from the neighbors if you keep down.”

“I will.”

He found his daily chore of caring for the little rabbit enjoyable. When he arrived it would jump about, twitching its nose, as if it was happy to see him. He would take it out of the cage and pet it. He decided to give it a name. From then on it would be known as *Twitchie,* from the way it wiggled its nose.

Jim noticed, with the shortage of food he'd lost all interest in sex, that had been such an important part of his life. With the idleness he was losing his self discipline which he had always prided himself on. He'd have to do something about it. First, he would start a daily routine of working out. Second, he'd start a journal of their daily events. Perhaps some day the family might enjoy reading it or he might even write a book about his life in hiding after the war.

Henceforth, every morning after visiting the privy he did Air Force calisthenics. He couldn't believe how out of shape he'd gotten sitting around. At first he puffed and wheezed, but gradually his stamina improved. The diary proved to be a challenge. So little happened it was hard to think what to write. But he religiously recorded the day's events no matter how mundane they might be.

One overcast night without a moon or stars, Nels unexpectedly showed up at the back door. There was no sign of the hoped for basket of food, but he did have a strange looking object, a dirty black box. Grinning like a Chessy Cat, he laid it on the kitchen table in front of the curious residents.

"You'll never believe what I've found."

They gathered around and stared at the nondescript article.

Nels carefully opened it. About the size of a shoe box it didn't look like much. "Look at this." He pulled out a brown metal rectangular object.

Jacob sneered, "What's all the fuss about? It's just an old box."

"It's an old fashioned radio. We found it in an abandoned farmhouse where we camped out one night."

Jim studied the radio. He was amazed at Nels' enthusiasm. It looked like an interesting antique, hardly of use to anybody. It was dirty and covered with rust.

Gretel asked, "Don't you have to plug it in? We don't have any power here, you know."

"It's battery operated. One of my lads found one that fits."

Nels switched it on and scanned the dial trying to find something. All they could hear was static and crackling. They could make out a woman singing in German.

Gretel smiled, "Can you believe that? It's in German, probably out of Hamburg."

Nels searched the dial again, discouraged when he couldn't get anything more interesting. Jim looked it over more carefully, "Look here. There's a terminal for an aerial. It needs an aerial."

Jacob growled, "Where are you gonna get one of those. It's useless."

Nels ignored his sarcasm, "Gretel, do you have any wire that might do the trick?"

"Let me think. My husband had a radio some years ago. I remember he had an aerial strung up in the attic. It might still be up there."

Nels looked excited, "Let's take a look. Maybe it will work after all."

Gretel rummaged through the kitchen cabinets looking for a flashlight.

Jacob got interested, "You know what. I took that out the other night looking for firewood. It's in the dining room buffet. I'll get it." He rushed into the other room, retrieved the flashlight and brought it back to Nels. He thought he might be able to find some German news and really find out what was going on in the war.

Gretel led the way to her bedroom. "Here, give me a hand. There's a door behind this bureau. I haven't been up there for years."

The men shoved it aside revealing a door behind the chest of drawers. It was securely locked with a rusty padlock. She took a key from her key ring and struggled to unlock it. Succeeding, she led the way up the wooden stairs to the dark and dusty attic. Jacob scanned the darkness with the flashlight. All they could see were old trunks covered with dust and cobwebs. She moved confidently over to a corner and located a thin copper wire connected to two rafters. "Here it is, just like I said. We'll need some pliers to cut it down. Jake, could you get the pliers? They're in the kitchen."

He grumbled, "I suppose I could."

Waiting for the slow moving Jacob, Jim wondered what stories and family history might be hidden in the attic. The house was hundreds of years old. Gretel had said she had lived there all of her life, and before that her grandparents. His reverie was interrupted when Jacob showed up with the pliers. Jim helped cut the wire down and they pulled it out and coiled it into a loop. They trooped back to the kitchen, eager to try it out with the radio. Nels attached it to the terminal on the radio and strung it across the room to a picture hanger, then turned the power on and searched the dial for a signal. He located a weak one from Berlin. It was a government station describing the glories of the German military and their latest victories.

Jim said, "It's just propaganda."

Gretel added, "What victories, they're on the defensive now."

"Never underestimate the Wehrmacht." Jacob said.

Nels tired of the routine propaganda and searched the dial again only to find a strong signal from Great Britain.

"Listen to this. I think it's the B.B.C. news broadcast.

> *"June 6, 1944. The Allies have landed at Normandy. The invasion of the continent is underway. They have encountered stiff resistance on the beaches."*

With the news of the long awaited invasion their spirits soared. Somehow the day-to-day routine and food shortages seemed more bearable, with renewed hope of liberation from the dreaded enemy. But as time passed the invasion stalled and the monotonous routine resumed. Jim found Jacob even more difficult. He tried to avoid contact with him but they did share the dinner table each night. Gretel sensed the antagonism and did her best to keep the peace.

The days passed interminably. After the excitement of the invasion the mood was bleak. Even with the onset of spring, when the weather improved, they suffered from the food shortages.

In August they listened to another broadcast. The Allies had broken out of Normandy and were sweeping across France. On August 23rd Paris was liberated. Spirits soared once more in the dreary old house.

Jim looked forward to his daily visits out back to care for the little rabbit. Now he didn't just feed him, but held Twitchie in his arms and stroked it affectionately. The news continued to be encouraging but often there were setabacks as well. In July a group of German officers had attempted to assassinate Hitler but the plot failed. The conspirators were all tortured and executed.

Later that year the news of the B.B.C. broadcast of December 16th was shocking. The Germans had mounted a massive counterattack in the Ardennes Forest region of France and Belgium. After the end of the war seemed so close it seemed impossible. It was called the Battle of the Bulge. German tank columns had surged forward with little resistance. Perhaps it was only a last desperate attempt to stave off defeat. Bastogne was surrounded and the Americans were unable to employ their air superiority due to bad weather.

As Christmas approached, one wintry morning, after an austere breakfast of brown bread and black coffee, Gretel asked Jim to join her in the parlor for a talk. Fearing bad news he followed her into the dark room. It was unusual for her to be so secretive.

"Captain Scott, you know how short of food we are. It's impossible to provide an adequate diet for you two men. Well, with Christmas approaching I'd like to prepare a real Christmas dinner for you two. Nels said he might join us."

"What did you want to tell me?"

Blushing, she added, "You won't like what I'm about to say."

"What is it, for gosh sake?"

"Well, it's about that little rabbit. I heard you gave it a name. What do you call it?"

"Twitchie."

"I guess I never got around to telling you. This is difficult to say. You won't like it. I'd been raising it for food, for meat, you know."

"Meat?" He turned beet red. "I don't believe it. I thought it was your pet."

She looked determined, "We can't afford pets now. We don't have time for such sentimentality."

Jim grimaced. She was probably right, but it was the one thing that had made his confinement more bearable. The thought of eating the poor little thing seemed almost barbaric.

He raised his voice, "That's the most sadistic thing I've ever heard."

"I don't know what that word means, but that's exactly what we're going to do."

Jim was astonished. This was his first disagreement with Gretel, a woman who he owed so much. Somehow he knew it was hopeless to argue with her. After all, it was her house and the rabbit belonged to her. "I suppose it'll have to be what you've decided, but I won't eat any of that meat."

"Now sir, I haven't asked you to do much around here. You've had your fun with the rabbit. I want you to butcher and dress it so we can have a real Christmas. You know how little meat we've had."

"Butcher it!" He almost shouted. "I couldn't do anything like that. He's my little buddy."

"Your little buddy. Now I've heard everything. What kind of talk is that for a grown man, an officer in the U. S. Army?"

"Let Jacob do it. It wouldn't bother him."

"He's too busy." Jim wondered what he was busy doing. All he ever did was dress up and sit around reading old books and smoking his pipe.

She did everything for him, waited on him like a dependant husband. The argument was fruitless. She'd made up her mind. He'd have to do it. He had to be careful what he said.

"I'll do it, if you insist." He grumbled.

Gretel thanked him and immediately left the room. She had won their first argument.

Maybe he was acting childish. As a boy on his grandfather's farm he'd butchered many chickens. He'd take the hatchet, catch the squawking chicken and take it out behind the barn and deliver the lethal blow. The beheaded chicken would flop hopelessly around spurting blood. The worst part was dousing it with boiling water to loosen the feathers. The stench was overpowering. Then he'd pluck the feathers and take it into the kitchen to his grandmother ready for the oven. He never had any trouble eating that meat.

As Christmas approached, Gretel didn't say another word about the rabbit. The day before Christmas he trudged grimly back to the pen. Twitchie was delighted to see him, jumping about in anticipation. He picked it up, grabbed the hatchet and headed back behind the privy where nobody could see him. The poor little thing seemed to almost anticipate its fate. Holding it down he delivered the blow to its neck. Jim would never forget the look of abject fear in its eyes. He'd never dressed a rabbit before, but with some helpful tips from Gretel he completed the grisly task.

Christmas morning dawned bright and sunny with clean fresh snow covering the ground. Gretel was humming Christmas carols in the kitchen preparing hasenpfeffer, a fine rabbit stew with potatoes, carrots and onions she had been hoarding for the holiday.

Jim was pleased to see her happy. He spent contented hours sitting by the fire smelling the aroma of the dish cooking on the stove. The Germans did not patrol that day and for once happiness prevailed in the house.

Nels arrived late in the afternoon, surprisingly clean and well dressed. Even Jacob and his dog seemed happy with the proceedings. Gretel had set the table in the seldom used dining room with her family china. When they sat down, Jacob, grinning mysteriously, went back to their bedroom and unearthed a bottle of red wine and brought it back to the amazed gathering. With a flourish, he took down four dusty crystal glasses, wiped them clean, and ceremoniously poured glasses of aged red wine for everybody.

For the moment the antagonisms of past months were put aside in holiday good cheer.

Jim raised his glass in a toast, “Here’s to our charming hostess who has prepared this wonderful feast for us. May the coming year bring victory and liberation for the people of Holland.”

They clicked their glasses in agreement.

After they started eating, Jim asked, “Nels, how come you risked coming out in daylight?”

“Well, as you already know. I thought it’d be safe. The Germans aren’t out tonight. Can you believe it they celebrate Christmas too?

“How about the collaborators?”

“I was careful no one saw me. I could always go down with you if they did come.”

Jacob eked out another round as Gretel served generous portions of the rabbit stew. Jim forgot about his reservations and enjoyed the meal with the others. They sopped up every ounce of the gravy with the bread. As the final *coup de grace*, Gretel brought out a hot mince pie which they happily consumed with their coffee.

Mellowing, with his second glass, Jacob leaned back in his chair. “You know, Nels, I had a substantial import-export business before the war. We had a large warehouse in Antwerp and two ocean going vessels. I had a good partner, but he made the mistake of resisting the occupation. If it hadn’t been for him we’d still be going. We imported textiles, China and Chinese Art from the Far East and exported cheese, tulip bulbs and other items to both China and Japan. We had some of the largest department stores in Europe as customers.

Jim was fascinated. It was the first time Jacob had talked about his past life. “I heard you had done well. What happened to the business and all that money?”

“We couldn’t get into or out of Japan after the Pacific war started and then the Germans seized all our assets, including the ships.”

“How’d that happen? I thought you got along with them.”

“My partner was found out and they wouldn’t listen to me.”

“How’d you happen to come to Groot?”

“I knew Gretel and her family before the war. When her husband died, she was nice enough to take me in.”

Jim thought, now he was living off of her with nothing to offer in return except sex. Thoughts of his crew and their fate intruded. He thought they were all right but he wished he had definite news of their safety.

Jacob added, “I used to travel a lot. Had some wonderful trips to the Far East.”

"Sort of a fringe benefit?"

"That's right. Plenty of wine, women and song, like you Americans say."

Gretel flushed and rushed back into the kitchen, alone with her thoughts.

Nels glanced at his watch and rose abruptly, "Well, gentlemen, I've got to be going. This has been a day to remember. Things are going better in the Ardennes. The sky finally cleared and airpower is turning the tide."

He stopped in the kitchen in time to give Gretel a warm embrace and kiss on the cheek, turned to Jim and shook his hand. "Goodbye, my friend. God be with you."

Nels slipped once more out into the dangers of the night.

CHAPTER XIII

"Those bastards got my friend Dale."

January, 1945; Groot, Holland

The day after Christmas Gretel went in town to the market, hopeful of finding some meat and fresh produce. As usual she was disappointed returning home with only a few black potatoes.

"Any news in town?" Jim asked.

"You won't believe this. They're tightening up again. The town's upset, but nobody dares say anything. They've started a curfew every night. Anyone caught out after eight will be arrested. They're using the church bell. It's a travesty. They must know they're losing the war."

"You'd think they would be letting up."

"That would be too reasonable. They don't think like normal people."

"You're probably right."

Several weeks later, they gathered around the radio after dinner for the B.B.C. broadcast. The Russians had advanced across Poland into Germany. The infamous concentration camp at Auschwitz was liberated. Just before the Russians got there the Nazis had forced thousands of the unfortunates into a death march to Germany so they could not be freed by the Russians.

For Jim the news was inconceivable. Back in the states he never liked the Jews too much, though he had become quite fond of his gunner, Finkenstadt. But these atrocities were beyond belief. The papers back home had hardly reported what was going on.

One cold January evening Nels came to the back door looking anxious and distraught, not the usually self confident fellow they were used to.

"What's wrong, Nels?" Jim asked.

Taking a deep breath, "We were distributing food to some of our supporters out near Brinkerhoff's farm. Those damned Nazis were able somehow to track us down. They ambushed us. We had to shoot our way out."

"Did you all get away?"

"No, they got my best friend Dale, shot him in the head. I got the bastard that did it. Ran for our lives. We were outmanned and outgunned. They had some heavy stuff, automatic weapons." He slumped in a chair.

"You were lucky to get away."

"I suppose, but poor Dale."

When Gretel came in she quickly sensed something was wrong. "What's happened? You look terrible."

Nels retold the story of the ambush and the death of Dale. Gretel was appalled, "I knew Dale as a boy growing up here. I'll fix you a nice cup of tea."

She hurried to put the teapot on stifling her tears.

Nels thought to change the subject. He never could stand seeing a woman cry. "I heard you were in town today. Anything new?"

"Have you heard about the curfew?"

"I heard. You better be extra careful. Don't go out at night at all. They're meaner than ever, taking out their reverses on the defenseless."

Jim's face was flushed with anger, "Those bastards. Isn't there something I can do? Could I join your group Nels?"

"That's out of the question. You'd stand out like a sore thumb. We're all Dutch, you know."

"I guess you're right. I'm getting claustrophobia sitting around here. But, I'm sure glad you made it back."

Nels announced, "Gretel, could you get Jacob in here?"

After he showed up, Nels said, "Now please listen carefully. The Germans are stepping up their searches. Somehow, they've found out we're using some of the houses for hiding. I don't know what it is, but the word is they've got some new tricks up their sleeves."

Gretel shuddered, "God help us."

"Remember to keep Jim's things together so he can grab them. Don't forget. If you've been eating, take his utensils down too."

"I never thought of that." Gretel said. "I admire you so much, taking such risks. Did you hear about the Russians? About Auschwitz and the death march?"

"I heard all about it. They forced them all, women and children, to walk hundreds of miles in the bitter cold, without adequate food or clothing. If they fell down they beat them to death."

Jim was trying to come to grips with the brutality of it all. He realized now he hadn't known anything about the oppression of the Jews.

Nels got up, "I've got to go."

He hurried out the back door and into the dangers of the night.

The house settled back into its usual routine. Jim was bored with the inaction but realized how lucky he was with his buddies in the Eighth still risking their necks every day.

One dark night a few weeks later, Nels unexpectedly appeared after their meager meal. He hurried in and warmed himself by the stove.

Jim greeted his friend, "I didn't expect you. It's such a lousy night."

"How're you doing?"

"We're all right. Had a close one last week. They were making their rounds, it seemed routine. Instead of stopping up the street they came directly here. They didn't find anything though."

"I don't like the sound of that. Maybe there's a leak. If they knew for sure somebody was here they'd burn the house down."

"I'd get a couple of them before they did that."

"Listen, Jim. I've got an idea. It's quiet tonight. I don't know what they're up to, but there's no one around. If you're willing, I'll take you out with me. Remember, you'll be safer here."

Jim brightened up, "Would you really? Just a minute I'll get my heavy sweater."

He rushed back to his room and bumped into Gretel on the way back.

"Where are you going? She asked.

"Nels said it was better if you didn't know."

They slipped out the back door. Crouching down, they ran from house to house, careful to stay in the shadows. It was a dark night which worked to their advantage. Safely, out of town Nels led the way at a frenetic pace with Jim struggling to keep up. After ten or fifteen minutes he stopped and retrieved two old bikes from the bushes.

"Here, mount up. It's a long way yet."

After they pedaled several miles Nels dismounted and led the way into the brush where they hid the bikes.

"Follow me." They walked together into the deep woods and came to a clearing where a group of men were gathered. Nels introduced Jim to the resistance fighters. They spoke only Dutch but greeted him cordially. When he got to the oldest man, Nels said, "Captain Scott, meet Dieter Lindenmuth, our leader."

Lindenmuth looked to be about fifty, lean and wiry, with powerful shoulders and arms. He had a look of authority and intelligence about him. He grasped Jim's hand with an iron grip, and in good English said, "Well, Captain, I'm happy to see you're one pilot the Krauts didn't get."

Jim grinned, "Thanks to Nels and your organization."

"Now, Captain . . . ."

"Please, call me Jim."

"It'll be Jim from now on. Now, Jim, I want to show you something, one of our best kept secrets. Would you follow me?"

Dieter led the way on a trail deeper into the woods. Hidden behind some dense bushes and carefully concealed Jim could see a camouflaged wooden shack. Dieter opened the door, lit a candle, and once they were both inside, closed the door behind them. The small musty room was furnished with a crude wooden table, two chairs and some assorted gear that looked like telephone equipment.

He pointed at the apparatus, "What do you think? It looks like Bell Telephone, doesn't it?"

Jim chuckled at the little joke, "What's this for anyway?"

"I was just about to tell you. We've strung a line underground from here to the British positions way south of here. For the first time we can coordinate our operations with the Brits."

"It's hard to believe. How could you ever do that?"

"It wasn't easy. We had a lot of help from some farmers. The hard part was getting it through the German lines."

"Sir, what an accomplishment. My hat's off to you."

"How would you like to talk to them?"

"Would I? You bet." Jim thought he might be able to get a message to his family who probably thought he was dead.

Dieter sat down and cranked the handle on the military type set. With the headphones on he cranked and cranked with no apparent result. Finally, he picked up some static and he could just make out a British voice. Jim could barely hear it. For him the scene was almost surreal, all of this happening with flickering candle light in this beat up old shack.

Dieter shouted into the microphone, "Hello, hello there. Do you read me?"

"I do. This is First Lieutenant Armbrust, Third Brigade, His Majesty's Army."

"Hello there, Armbrust. How are you tonight? This is Dieter Lindenmuth, Dutch Underground."

"Listen Armbrust, we've got an American pilot here we've been protecting. Had to bail out near the Zuider Zee when his engines failed in his bomber. He'd like to talk to you. Can I put him on?"

"Certainly, Dieter."

He handed the mike over to Jim. "Hello, Lieutenant Armbrust. How are you tonight?"

"How can I help you, lad?"

"Could you tell me? Are you planning to move up soon?"

"Sorry. I couldn't tell you even if I knew. But we are building up our forces."

"That sounds encouraging. It can't be too soon. It's getting worse here."

"I'm worried sick about my family. They might think I'm dead. I'm sure the Pentagon has reported me missing in action."

"I'll pass the word through channels. But they won't report your status. It's against policy."

"What policy? What kind of policy is that?"

"Your government's policy. It would endanger the boys in hiding, let alone the Dutch underground. Any other requests?"

"How far are you from here?

"I can't tell you over the wire. You never know."

"Why don't you guys move up? I heard the Germans are thin in this sector."

"Maybe so, but you know the brass. We're awaiting our orders. You're a military man, you will understand."

"Can't they speed it up?"

"Monty's the best judge of that. I'm sure there's some tactical reason. I'll have to sign off now. Nice to talk to you."

Dieter grabbed the mike before Jim could hang up. He shouted, "Couldn't the R.A.F. drop some food? We're desperately short."

"I'll pass the word along. See what the air lads can do. Most of our bombers are busy bombing Germany."

"I appreciate that. But see what you can do about the food."

"I promise. Jolly good talking to you. Keep up the good work."

They hurried back on the trail to rejoin the other men. Jim turned to the top man, "Thanks a lot Mr. Lindenmuth. It was great talking to the British."

Nels said, "We've got to go now, Jim."

They walked silently back to the bikes and rode back through the darkness to Groot. Nels hid the bikes just before they got to town and they carefully walked in the shadows to the safe house. At the door Jim thanked Nels profusely and watched as he walked back into the night. He wondered what it was like being a young freedom fighter, never knowing if you'd live from one day to the next.

He went back to his cold bedroom, quickly shed his pants and sweater and crawled under the heavy woolen blanket, his mind percolating with happy thoughts and his hope for the coming freedom for Holland from the heavy hand of the Nazis.

CHAPTER XIV

"Fang trotted obediently along in a posture of newfound respect."

February, 1945; Groot, Holland

The excitement of the night's outing quickly passed and the tedious routine of life in hiding settled in like a wet blanket. Gretel was busy with her household chores and Jacob was more remote. Jim thought about his dilemma and decided he'd make one more effort to draw Jacob out. Perhaps they could have some sort of relationship after all.

One day after their usual breakfast he drew his chair closer to the unfriendly Dutchman. "Mr. Schimmel, could you tell me something more about your business before the war. I don't think I told you. My dad had a small store in the states. He might have sold some of the things you handled.

Jacob smiled scornfully, "Those little stores don't amount to much. We had a real business, made millions.

"I'm sure you did. Weren't you an importer?"

"That's right. I told you that before."

"I guess you did."

"What kind of goods did you handle?"

"Fabrics: silk and cotton, fine glassware, Chinese Porcelain, vases and lamps."

"How'd you sell those products?"

"We dealt with some of the finest department stores in Europe."

"Why did they favor imports?"

"You Yanks are so damned ignorant. Don't you know anything about business?"

By this time Jim was incensed, almost unable to control himself. "I was studying history, can't you remember?"

"It was the prices. No one could make those products here for competitive prices. The Germans confiscated everything. If it hadn't been for what my partner did we'd still be in business."

"No wonder you're down."

His face reddened, "Down, down! There's nothing wrong with my spirit. I'll get it all back some day. What business is it of yours anyway? You're only here for a short time. We're the ones who are suffering. Stay away from me. I can't stand the sound of your voice."

Jim persevered, "Let me ask you something. It's been bothering me ever since I got here. Why don't you want me here? I haven't done anything to you."

Jacob shouted, "Done, what have you done? You're a damned fool. We're short of food because of you. If the Nazis find you it's all over. We'd be shot for harboring an American spy."

"So that's it. Listen, it's because of me the underground helps to feed you."

"We were getting along fine before you came here. With all these inspections we're in terrible danger. You are only here because of her misguided patriotism. If she'd just accept the occupation, we'd be all right."

"You want her to be a collaborator? She'd never do that. Our air force is helping win the war. Soon, you'll have your country back."

"You and your stupid questions. Just leave me alone. You're here and there's nothing I can do about it."

"If that's the way you want it. That's the way it will be. You are the most arrogant and overbearing man I ever met." Jim got up and left the room, concerned that he might have said too much.

Jim's run-ins with the rottweiler hadn't improved. It was almost impossible to beat him to the rocker. Jacob thought it was highly amusing. When the rotten dog bared its teeth, Jim ended up sitting on a hard wooden bench.

One evening later in the month, Nels showed up for one of his now rare visits. Jim jumped up when he heard the muffled knocking on the back door.

"Hi, Nels. Am I glad to see you? I've started talking to myself."

"Hello. What's bothering you? You don't look too well."

"It's that son-of-a-bitch Jacob. He's the most difficult man I ever met. He obviously doesn't want me around here. Makes no bones about it."

"Don't worry about it. It doesn't matter what he thinks. It's Gretel's house. If it weren't for her I'd get him out of here."

"What does she see in him? Could it be sex?"

"That's hard to believe. Listen, it's a dark night. Let's take a little walk. Maybe, it will calm you down."

"I'd love to go."

"Here, Fang. Let's go boy."

He jumped up, ready for a lark. Jim couldn't believe it. "Do we have to take him?"

"He might help us. Dogs have this acute sense of hearing. He might hear something we couldn't"

"Good idea. Let's go."

They cautiously slipped from house to house in the darkness. When they got out of town Nels took off at a fast pace. For Jim it was a rare treat to be enjoyed. Watching the dog happily trotting along by Nels, he had a brainstorm. "Nels, could you hold up for a minute. I've got to take a leak. I'll go back there in the woods."

Nels stopped. What a strange thing this American had to have privacy when he relieved himself.

Jim called, "Here boy, here boy."

The surprised dog jumped up, amazed at the attention.

Jim led the way, as Fang darted along sniffing every tree and marking them with his urine. Nature called and he squatted down. It was the chance Jim had been looking for. With his heavy boots, he delivered a vicious kick to the dog's rear end, right on his balls. The dog writhed in pain letting out pathetic whimpers. The chastened dog trailed along behind in a posture of newfound respect.

Nels couldn't help but notice the changed demeanor. What's wrong with that dog? Why's he acting like that?"

"Like what? I didn't notice anything. Let's get going."

"He looks like he likes you. I thought he didn't like you. What are you grinning about?"

"Maybe, he liked me taking him for a walk."

Nels knew something had happened, but it was certain that Jim wasn't going to tell him.

When they got back to the safe house Nels hurried to say his goodbyes and leave. Jim went back to his bedroom, pleased with himself, his mind busy with happy thoughts. It was sort of dumb to be preoccupied with such trivialities but wasn't success wonderful. He slept like a log that night.

CHAPTER XV

"If you make one false move, you're a dead man."

Later in February, 1945; Groot, Holland

Some weeks later after the incident with Fang the unlikely threesome gathered after dinner in the kitchen. Gretel retrieved the radio from its hiding place underneath the bench and hooked up the aerial. Spinning the dial she located the B.B.C. She was pleased when she found a hopeful song about the war.

There'll be blue birds over
The white cliffs of Dover
Tomorrow
Just you wait and see . . . .

"What a wonderful song. It gives you hope that one day this terrible war will be over and we can go back to everyday lives."

Jim added, "We can all agree on that."

Jacob didn't say a word, keeping his thoughts to himself.

Then the news came on. It told once more about the infamous concentration camp, Auschwitz, that had been liberated by the advancing Russian armies and that thousands died in the death march into Germany.

Gretel teared up, "What kind of monsters would do a thing like that?"

Jim choked up, the enormity of the crimes against humanity finally coming home to him.

Jacob was unmoved, "You don't believe that, do you? Most of those Jews are Communists anyway. They stirred up all kinds of trouble before the war."

Jim answered, "Surely, you don't go along with that. That's just Nazis propaganda.

Jacob scowled, and quickly left the room for fear that Gretel would get upset with him.

February, that fateful year proved to be one of the coldest on record. The Dutch suffered grievously. The Nazis were even more brutal as their fortunes waned. With the lack of heat in the stone house, Jim spent most of his time in the kitchen by the little wood fire. He often slept with his clothes on, with a heavy sweater to keep his chest warm. The concrete floor in the former garage was like a slab of ice. The worst ordeal was going out back to the privy.

Gretel heard in town that the Dutch dairy herds had been moved by ship to escape the enemy. Dairy products: cheese, butter and milk had always been a mainstay of their diet. Now, they were almost nonexistent. One bitter night Nels arrived unexpectedly at the back door looking tired.

"The Nazis are cracking down. It's going to be tougher than ever, I'm sorry to say."

Gretel grimaced, "What can they do they're not already doing."

Nels said, "These men don't have any future. They know that. Most of them are from occupied countries where they can't go back. They're traitors in their own homeland."

Jim asked, "How're they tightening up?"

"They're stepping up the searches. And worst of all they've got a well trained police dog."

"Can't they leave us alone? The war's almost over." Gretel said.

Jacob said, "I told you all along. We're in terrible danger with the Yank here. They'll find him now with that dog. You know what they'll do to us if they find him. Come to your senses, Gretel, get him out of here."

Jim had thought all along it might come to this. "He's right, you know. I'll leave and you will be safe."

"Where would you go?" Gretel asked.

"I'll go out in the country, hide in the woods. I'll find an abandoned barn for shelter. I had lots of experience camping out back home. I owe you and Nels so much. I'll be all right."

Nels shot back, "That's ridiculous, you'd freeze to death. We are honor bound to protect you."

"That dog will find me for sure. Then it will be the end for all of us. Think about it, Nels."

"Hide some meat at strategic places. The dog will forget all about the search. We've done that before."

"Do you think it will work?" Gretel asked.

"You never know for sure, but it's the best chance we have. There's no way I won't protect Jim, with all the United States is doing to win the war."

Jacob raised his voice, "Turn him over. Get him out of here. It's the only thing to do. We can claim he surreptitiously came in the back door or one of the windows." He jumped up and started toward Jim.

Nels fingered his Lugar, "Listen, Jacob. If you make one false move you're a dead man.

"Calm down Nels. I didn't mean anything. I'll go along with what you say. You're in charge."

Nels got up and walked over in front of Jacob and looked him in the eye, "Now, you son-of-a-bitch, remember what I said. Your idea is ridiculous. The Nazis would never believe he got in here uninvited."

Jacob mumbled almost inaudibly, "You're right, Nels, I'll do anything you say."

The tension lessened when Nels took his leave. Jim was satisfied Jacob wouldn't do anything stupid.

The ensuing nights were the worst of all. It seemed like there were patrols almost every night. Before they were predictable, but now they came unexpectedly, at odd times, sometimes in the middle of the night.

They took turns on watch. Jacob looked drawn. He had lost his composure and assumed superiority. Jim, with his combat experience, looked confident and Gretel went about her chores as if nothing was happening. She had long since accepted the possibility of death at the hands of the Germans. Perhaps it would be a relief after the way they were living.

One night Jim was on watch after the others went to bed. Half asleep, he roused with a start when he heard the sound of a lorry. He rushed to wake Gretel and Jacob.

"Gretel, Jacob, wake up! They're coming. They're right up the street. Hurry!"

Jim ran to his room, gathered up his few belongings, and raced to the bench where he threw them down into the gloom. He climbed quickly down with his Colt 45 at the ready. Jacob and Gretel worked feverishly to erase any tell tale signs of Jim's presence. They finished just in time when the lorry pulled up in front of the house. They heard the threatening sound of the trooper's boots as they stomped to the front door.

"Bang! Bang! Bang!" The heavy oak door shook with the pounding.

Jacob went back into their bedroom where he feigned a nap. Gretel smoothed her hair, straightened her dress and slowly walked through the parlor to the front door. She deliberately slid the bolt back and opened the door a crack. A burly red-faced non-com shoved her aside and demanded, "What's the idea? You open this door immediately, is that clear?"

"Yes, yes sir. I will. I couldn't hear you in the kitchen."

Two young troopers charged in right behind him with guns mounted. A fourth German followed with a black German shepherd on a leash. The snarling animal sniffed out every inch in the front room but failed to find anything. They all rushed into the kitchen where Fang was sleeping peacefully by the fire. He jumped up at the sight of the other dog and tentatively wagged his tail. The shepherd ignored his entreaties and sniffed around the kitchen. He found a piece of moldy meat and wolfed it down.

When the sergeant found Jacob on the bed he ordered, "Get up from there. Stand at attention."

Jacob quickly obeyed, "Yes sir, Sergeant. I support the occupation. I'm a friend. Holland was hopelessly weak and an ally of England."

"Enough of that. Get out of my way." He and an aide tore the bed apart, ransacked the room and emptied the drawers on the floor. Finding nothing they started back to Jim's room.

Meanwhile, back in the kitchen, Fang assumed a belligerent pose with his hair standing up. Down in the darkness Jim quietly cocked his pistol being careful to muffle the sound. Fang had enough; he charged the shepherd from behind, knocking it down with the violence of his attack. One of the troopers mounted his rifle, but watched helplessly as the two animals rolled on the floor in mortal combat. Soon the floor was covered with blood. Gretel was horrified when the German dog had Fang by the nape of the neck. Somehow he managed to extricate himself and went on the attack. The trooper squeezed off a shot but it ricocheted harmlessly off the stone floor. Now, Fang had the edge, shaking his enemy to and fro by the neck. But, he made the fateful mistake of backing off when he was exhausted and unable to continue the attack. The trooper took careful aim and shot the heroic dog through the head.

The trooper gathered the stricken shepherd in his arms and beat a hasty retreat, cursing all the time, out the front door to the lorry. As he went out the he bellowed, "We'll be back. We know you're up to something."

When the lorry went up the street Jim crawled out of the trench. He and Jacob carried the dead dog outside to the back of the yard. For once they agreed on something. Fang was a hero and deserved a proper send-off. He had only attacked when the shepherd discovered Jim's hiding place. They meticulously buried the dog and said a simple prayer in his honor. Jim marked the grave with a large stone.

What a turn of events, Fang, the dog that had harassed Jim for so long, had saved all of their lives.

CHAPTER XVI

"The most pathetic girl Jim had ever seen."

March, 1945; Groot, Holland

That fateful winter of 1944-1945 proved to be the most severe of the occupation. The brutal cold led to widespread starvation and deaths due to exhaustion and disease. It would come to be known as the hunger winter (Hungerwinter). The food shortages were aggravated by a general railroad strike instigated in late 1944 by the exiled Dutch government in England. They had anticipated an early end to the war and an end to the repressive Nazi regime.

Despite the encouraging news of the Allied advances, the situation in Gretel's household grew steadily worse. In town, she had heard of even more severe treatment of the Jews left in the country, as if the enemy wished to finally exterminate the Jewish race.

One unusually bitter night Nels arrived at the back door. He looked exhausted. Slumping in a kitchen chair he warmed his hands by the tiny flickering fire.

"Gretel, I've got to impose on you once more to help out. It's an emergency. We've rescued this little Jewish girl in Amsterdam. She's been in hiding. Her parents were taken away by the Nazis, probably to a death camp. The poor thing's half dead due to starvation. She'll die for sure or be picked up by the Germans if we don't find a place for her."

Gretel looked distressed, "You know Nels, I've heard all these stories about the Jews. It's hard to believe anybody could do these horrid things. Sure we'd like to help. But you must realize how short of food we are. We're wasting away. Look at Jim. He looks like a skeleton."

"I know what's happening. But I must implore you to help out. It's her only chance. Once you see her you'll know what I mean. We'll try to bring you more provisions."

Jim was genuinely moved. "It's not my place to decide, but I'll cut back on what I eat."

Jacob scowled, "That's outrageous. You'd ask this for a dirty little Jew?"

Nels stood up and assumed a threatening manner, "Listen, Jacob. You'll go along with whatever Gretel decides. You're a guest here yourself. Sit down and shut up."

Jacob scowled but slumped obediently in a chair.

"Now Gretel, we deeply appreciate all you've done. It's hard to ask you this, but I had to do it."

"Where is this girl? Could I see her?"

"She's hidden just outside of town."

"So Gretel doesn't have a choice. You've already decided." Jacob interjected.

Nels face reddened, "What'd I tell you, Jacob? Stay out of this."

"Go and get her. I'd like to see her before I decide." Gretel said.

Nels rose and gave Gretel a hug, and hurried out on his mission of mercy.

When the door closed, Jacob turned on Gretel. "This, my dear, is the most stupid thing you've done yet. We're already in grave danger with this Yank here. If they ever find us with a Jew, it'll be the end."

Jim flushed, "You heard what Nels said, you don't have any choice. It's up to Gretel."

She pleaded with Jacob, "Listen, dear, calm down. We'll be all right if I do decide to go along. We can hide her down below with Jim if there's a search. Nels said they'd bring more food. Let's just see what she looks like."

He knew it was hopeless to argue with her. She was the most stubborn woman he'd ever met.

Gretel busied herself fixing a pot of tea. It always seemed to calm men down. She couldn't stand all this wrangling. They sipped their tea in silence as they waited.

After about a half hour Nels returned with the most pathetic little black-haired and dark-eyed girl that Jim had ever seen.

Gretel took one look at the poor thing, half starved and emaciated, and announced, "I've decided. We'll take her in."

"Thank God. You've got a good heart," Nels said.

"I couldn't agree more. Something had to be done," Jim added.

"You'll regret this foolish decision. Where will she sleep? That spare bedroom is loaded with old furniture and boxes," Jacob said.

"We'll just have to clean it up. What's her name, Nels?"

"Sylvia Zimmerman."

Gretel approached the girl and extended her hand. "I'm pleased to meet you, Sylvia. You're welcome here."

She smiled appreciatively, but did not reply. Despite her forlorn appearance she seemed to realize she was in the hands of a warm and motherly woman, after all the months of hiding and peril.

Jacob stomped out of the room, thoroughly disgusted by the proceedings.

Sylvia was perhaps five feet tall with dark eyes and jet black hair. Her face was sunken, her tummy enlarged, and her tiny arms and legs emaciated. Gretel recognized the sure signs of partial starvation. She wrapped her in a warm embrace, as she muffled her tears.

"Here, my dear, take a seat." Gretel pulled a chair up and helped her to sit down. "I'm sure you could use a bit to eat. I'll get you something. Just sit here by the fire and warm yourself."

She poured her a cup of tea and brought out some dry biscuits from the cupboard.

The girl started to cry, overcome with the warmth of the welcome. When she recovered a bit, she devoured the biscuits, washing them down with the tepid tea. It was the first food she'd had in several days. But she was quickly overcome with a wave of nausea and threw up on the floor.

The smell of the vomit was disgusting. Gretel hastened to clean up the mess. She hated doing it, but she was a good housewife and couldn't tolerate anything like that in her house.

When she finished, she announced, "Now, Jim, if you would help me. We'll make a place for Sylvia."

Jim's basic humanity overcame his reservations. He put aside his early opinions of the Jews and quickly rose to assist Gretel in the charitable act.

Nels was moved by Gretel's concern for the unfortunate girl, and heartened by Gretel's compassion. He knew that the girl was in safe hands. He'd done his part, and was pleased with himself. At an opportune moment, he excused himself and disappeared out the back door. Somehow, acts like this made all of the hardship and danger worthwhile. He'd saved the child from sure death at the hands of the Nazis.

In the meantime Sylvia had fallen asleep sitting up in the chair, her head slumped to the side.

They each took an arm and helped her across the kitchen to the door of the spare bedroom. With her free hand Gretel opened the door, only to be greeted by a blast of cold musty air. By the light of a candle Jim could just make out a small cot over in the corner, piled high with boxes and old papers. They sat her down in a dusty easy chair, and Gretel found two woolen blankets in a chest of drawers to keep her warm.

"I'm afraid this'll have to do for now. I'll clean this up tomorrow. Now Jim, if you'd help me we'll put her to bed."

He went over and picked the girl up in his arms, astonished at how little she weighed, and laid her gently on the cot where Gretel covered her with the blankets. Sylvia was fast asleep as they left the room. They were exhausted by the strain of the day's events and ready for bed themselves.

When Gretel got to her bedroom, Jacob was already in bed, waiting to have it out with her. He started in, but sensing she was in no mood for an argument, decided to wait for a more opportune time. He'd have to think this situation through. His life and the security of his business were at stake, if the Germans ever discovered that Jew in the house.

Nels had brought a large basket of potatoes, shrunken apples and several cabbages. Sylvia couldn't keep any solid food down so Gretel sought to nourish her back to health with cabbage and potato soup and hot tea. The cabbage brought on an acute case of dysentery. She grew weaker, unable to even stand on her feet. Gretel restricted her diet to apple sauce, rice and tea. After several days it did the job and she gradually improved, regaining some of her strength. Caring for the girl was a round-the-clock effort. Gretel enjoyed her motherly role but felt worn out much of the time.

Jacob was even more sullen, scarcely saying a civil word to anyone. He bitterly resented the girl's presence and felt neglected, after losing all the attentions Gretel had showered on him. The only good thing for him was that Gretel was too worn out to seek their regular sexual intercourse. He was happy to be relieved of that odious duty that he had never enjoyed. He avoided going in to see Sylvia, and later on, when Jim carried her out by the fire, he'd go back to their bedroom to avoid her presence.

One evening when Jim had gone back to write in his journal, Jacob accosted Gretel in a nasty voice, "Just how long is this going on? We've been lucky so far. The patrols have let up. But they'll be back. We both know that. Come to your senses, woman. What good will it be if they find her and we're all killed. Even your friend Jim will be shot."

"Now, calm down, Jake. It's gonna be all right. Jim said if they came he'd carry her down with him. You and I can take care of the rest."

His face darkened, "That's nonsense and you know it. Just wishful thinking. It'll never work. How can you be so stubborn? You're just like your mother."

Gretel flushed scarlet, "MY MOTHER! How dare you bring up my mother, long dead in her grave. You've gone too far this time. I tell you I'm getting fed up with your negative thoughts. Compose yourself. This's the way it's going to be, whether you like it or not. Don't forget you're my guest in this house. If you don't like it, you can get out."

She took out a handkerchief to keep from crying in front of him. She had grown attached to the girl. She viewed caring for her as her mission. She had always thought of herself as a good Christian, and this was her chance to prove it to herself. Perhaps the relationship reminded her of the daughter she'd never had.

After a prolonged silence, she calmly added, "Now, Jake, we can work this out. I'm sorry what I said. I do want you here. You're my only love."

"Why'd you have to bring that up? I'm a guest. You begged me to come and stay with you. Remember?"

"I suppose I did, but don't wear out your welcome."

Jacob retreated into silence. He knew now it was impossible to change her mind. And he didn't have any other place to go. He couldn't wait until he got out of this prison, back to the life style he was accustomed to. He'd only made love to her to have a place to stay. Her fat body and crude ways disgusted him. He could hardly tolerate her presence in bed beside him, with her pathetic protestations of love.

More tired than ever, and upset about the argument with Jacob, she decided to ask Jim to help out. One morning after their meager breakfast, she said, "I've something to ask of you." This was hard for her. She wasn't used to asking anyone for help. "Do you suppose? Do you think you could help me out a little with the girl? I've got to admit I'm worn out."

"I wondered about that. You don't look like your usual self."

"Would you consider it? I know you wanted something to do."

He hesitated. He didn't like the thought of caring for Sylvia. He'd never done anything like that in his life, and he didn't think he'd be good at it. How would he get along with this girl? Despite his sympathy, her appearance was revolting and she even smelled bad.

Gretel sensed his hesitation. "Now, Jim, I've never asked you anything before."

He wrestled with his conscience. Down deep he knew it was the only thing he could do. With his strict upbringing, he'd always tried to do the right thing, whether he liked it or not. "I suppose I could feed her. I've got to help you; you've done so much for me."

"Thanks so much. I'll fix a tray tonight and you can take it in."

All day he wondered how he could handle this. What would it be like to have a friendly relationship with a Jewish girl?

That evening after their dinner in strained silence, Gretel fixed a tray with her hearty soup, two hard rolls and a mug of tea. He carried the tray into the darkened room, set it down on a table near the bed, and lit a candle. Sylvia was sound asleep. "Sylvia, Sylvia, wake up." She tentatively opened her eyes, startled to see Jim standing next to the bed.

She asked, "What's going on? Where's Gretel? Has something happened to her?"

"No! No! Nothing's happened. She just asked me to help out."

She sat up in the bed. "I'm not hungry. Please take it away."

"But you've got to eat, to build up your strength. Try this soup. It's good."

He dipped the spoon in the bowl and brought it to her mouth. "Please try this. You'll like it."

She meekly acquiesced, not knowing what else to do. He painstakingly fed her the soup, but she refused to eat the rolls, claiming she was full. But she did seem to enjoy the hot tea. He took the leftovers back to the kitchen, where Gretel put them back in the cupboard for future use.

Jacob was seated in his chair by the fire. "How's the little nurse? I heard you had some new duties."

"I'm pleased to help out."

With his most contemptuous look, "I'm sure you are. You don't seem to realize how much more danger we're in."

"For once you might be right. But remember this. It's Gretel's house. She's made a decision. This is the way it's gonna be. Without her and Nels we'd both be in trouble."

"Perhaps you're right, for once. But listen. She's just a despicable little Jew. She doesn't belong with us. She should be with her own people. They're different, you know."

"Listen to this, Jacob. You don't seem to get it. She has no place to go. Her family was taken away by the Nazis. If they find her, she'd end up in a concentration camp for sure. They put them in gas chambers. I'd think even you could see that."

"It serves them right. This will be a better country when they're all gone."

"You know, I've never liked the Jews at home too well myself. But then I had this really great gunner on my ship named Finkenstadt. Whatever you think of the race, how can you stomach exterminating millions of people. And Silvia, she's so pathetic and just a child. Don't you have any sympathy for the poor little thing?"

"No, I don't! Gretel should turn her over. We'd all be safer."

"She'll never do that. I don't think you understand Gretel at all. She's a warm compassionate person. She hates the Nazis. She's risking her own life every day to fight back."

Jacob was getting more and more irritated with these arguments. "She's making a big mistake. If she'd only try to understand the German point of view."

Jim felt a surge of blood to his head. "Point of view! Point of view! Hitler overran Europe. Murdered millions. All in the name of lebensraum, whatever that is."

"You'll never understand. You Americans are so naïve. You don't appreciate what happened in Germany. The Jews controlled most of the capital. The Reds were about to take over. Hitler saved the country. If it hadn't been for him, the Communists would have succeeded. You're not a Communist, are you?"

Jim raised his voice indignantly, "What the hell are you talking about? I serve in the U.S. Air Force. Of course I'm not a Communist. Come to your senses, man. Germany is losing this war. It'll be just a matter of time now. When Hitler invaded Russia and the U.S. came in, he didn't have a chance."

Jacob stomped out of the room. He'd had enough arguing with this naïve American, who was so stupid.

Jim was worried. He couldn't figure out this hard-head who wouldn't listen to logic. After all, they'd taken his business and he was destitute. He wondered what he might do now. Surely, he wouldn't turn over the girl. What would he have to gain? If he did, they'd all be at risk. The Nazis would believe he was helping Gretel shelter the Jew. What he couldn't figure out was how such a fine woman could sleep with such a bastard. Jim had never thought he could understand women, even the ones he admired so much, like Gretel.

Jacob grew more morose and belligerent. He scarcely ever spoke to Jim and resented all the time that Gretel spent with the girl. Luckily, there weren't any more inspections, but they were sure to come. It was only a matter of time. He had to come up with something. He decided to appeal to Nels. Perhaps he would be more reasonable.

Nel's visits were more infrequent. With the acute food shortages in the land, it was harder to find supplies. He had little time for the social visits he had enjoyed so much. But he thought he'd better stop by to see if Jacob had calmed down and was going along with Sylvia being there. So one night he arrived at the back of the house. When Gretel answered the door, she was surprised to see him. "Nels, how are you? We've been worried, wondering what happened to you. This is great. Come in."

"Sorry to say, this isn't a social visit. Times are so tough. I wanted to see how you were getting along with Sylvia and what Jacob was doing. Has he been all right?"

"It hasn't been too good. He's very difficult. The poor dear. I've been spending so much time with Silvia he feels neglected."

"I'd like to talk to him privately."

She went back to their bedroom and woke Jacob from his nap. Jim was back in his room writing in his journal. When Jacob came in Nels greeted him coldly.

"I've been wanting to talk to you, Nels. It's about this girl, Sylvia. We've been very fortunate so far. The Nazis haven't been on the street. But it's only a matter of time. There's no way we can get her down below quick enough with all of the evidence. Can't you do something? I can't even talk to Gretel about it. You know how stubborn she can be."

"I don't think she's stubborn at all. She's doing the right thing. I admire her for it. I know there's danger, but it's a necessary danger. What would you have her do? Turn her over for certain death?"

"You're damned right I would. It's the only thing to do. If the Nazis find her here, we'll be killed."

Nels face reddened. He raised his voice, "You're not worried about anybody else. Just yourself. You know what I told you the last time. You better shut up."

"I might turn her over myself."

Nels stood up, assumed a menacing manner, and shouted, "Listen to this, Jacob Schimmel, if you ever do that, I'll shoot you myself."

With this Jacob slumped in his chair and quieted down. "All right, Nels, I'm sorry I said that. I didn't mean it."

Nels barked, "Go back and get Jim, I want to talk to him privately."

Jacob hurried to obey, genuinely worried for the first time. He should probably be more careful what he said.

When Jim came in, he realized there had been a problem. "What's going on, my friend? Jacob looks like the devil. You don't look so good yourself."

"It's just Jacob. It's getting worse. He even threatened to turn Sylvia over himself. If he ever does that, I'll get him."

"I'm worried, too. I'll keep my eye on him. I don't think even he is that stupid. They'd shoot us all, him included."

"You're probably right. But we'd better be careful. If you see anything suspicious, let me know. I've got to go now. The situation's getting desperate. Many people are starving. I'm sorry I can't get something for you. But I'll keep trying. So long for now."

Nels hastened out the door into the night and the terrible dangers that he faced. Jim was left with his thoughts and the responsibility of watching Jacob. He'd been so lucky being here with the kind and loving Gretel, but living under the same roof with old Jacob was his cross to bear, as they used to say at church back home.

As the days passed, the situation with Jacob grew even more difficult. Now he refused to talk to Jim at all, so Jim had no way of knowing what he was thinking. The only good thing was that he didn't make any more threats about Sylvia. Perhaps Nels had scared him enough to keep him quiet. Jim found helping out made him feel needed and useful to his friend, Gretel. As Sylvia gained strength they had some interesting conversations.

One evening he brought in her tray. She actually smiled at seeing him. "You know what, Captain; I'm feeling a little better."

"That's good to hear."

"I've been so lucky, Nels bringing me here. You and Gretel have been so good to me. I hope that my being here doesn't endanger the rest of you."

"We'll be all right."

"Who's that big man I saw when I first was brought here? I haven't seen him since. I just had a feeling he wasn't to be trusted."

"He's a friend of Gretel's."

"Are they married?"

"No, they aren't. He's just a friend."

"What's he doing here, anyway?"

"She's helping him out. He didn't have any place to go. He lived in Amsterdam. The Nazis seized his business and his house. He grew up here and came back to Groot to ride out the occupation. There's something I'd like to ask you. Please don't take offense. I heard you were in hiding in the city, but the Nazis were getting too close. Nels said they got you out and brought you here to save your life. What happened to the rest of your family?"

"Didn't you know? They called them into the street, all the men in our neighborhood. They were told they were going to be moved to another location and to bring all their necessary personal belongings. It didn't sound too bad, so they went along willingly. Papa never seemed concerned about himself, just Mother and me. Later they took Mother and my brother. I was left behind."

"Did you ever hear anything more about your parents?"

"I was told they were loaded into trucks and later trains and taken to a concentration camp. I haven't heard a word since." With this she started to cry pathetically.

"Please don't cry. I'm sure they'll be all right. We'll just have to make the best of this situation until the war's over. We listen to the BBC broadcasts. The news is encouraging. The Allies are advancing across France. Paris has been liberated. I'm sure the Germans are losing. It'll only be a matter of time. I've got to go now. I've been keeping this journal. Your being here gives me something interesting to write about. See you tomorrow."

"Do you have to go so soon?"

"I really should. I'm afraid I'll wear you out with all this talking."

"Goodbye. Will I see you tomorrow?

"Don't worry, little girl, I'll be here."

Sylvia had never had a friendship with a Gentile, growing up in Amsterdam. Her family was very strict orthodox Jews and didn't believe in associating with people of other religions. It was difficult understanding their viewpoints, but what was she to do? They were so nice and helping her in her time of need. Even weakened as she was, she recognized how fortunate she'd been in being rescued by the underground and being brought to this house with these kind people. But she was overwhelmed with fear at the thought of her Mom and Dad. Her only hope was the war would end in time and they would be rescued.

She lived on hope, hope the war would quickly end, and hope her family would be together again.

CHAPTER XVII

"For now he'd have to keep his mouth shut."

February-March; Groot, Holland

Jim found caring for the half-starved Jewish girl rewarding. For the first time since he arrived at Gretel's house he felt needed, and he had someone intelligent to talk to. Any reservations he had about their different religions were swept aside with their newfound friendship. As she gained strength and felt better she seemed to enjoy talking to him. Gretel was so busy with her housework, trying to find enough food for the larger group, that she scarcely had time for a friendly word. But she enjoyed seeing Jim's changed attitudes. She remembered how Jim had felt about the Jewish race when he first came, and what he was now doing for Sylvia. Jacob grew more depressed and hostile, hardly even agreeable with Gretel. His hatred of the little Jew obsessed him. Most of all, he was afraid. He thought only of himself not that concerned even for his protector Gretel.

One night Nels showed up out back with alarming news. With Jim and Gretel present, he announced, "My friends, I've some bad news. The word is out that the Nazis suspect that a Jewish girl who escaped from Rotterdam is in hiding in this town. They're going to tighten up again. Anyone involved in protecting her will be shot on sight."

In the hallway, Jacob had overheard Nels' revelation. He stepped into the kitchen, his face contorted: "Now you've done it. They're getting closer every day. They'll be on to you soon. We'll all be held responsible. Nels, would you get her out of here?"

"No, I won't. I told you before. This is Gretel's house. It's up to her. What do you say, Gretel?"

"I'll tell you something for sure, Jacob. She's staying here as long as I'm alive. You'll just have to put up with it. If you don't like it, you can get out."

"I never thought you'd talk to me like that, my dear. You know how fond I am of you. It's just that you're making a terrible mistake."

"I might be, but that's the way I feel."

Jacob slumped in a chair. He realized he'd never change her mind. The die was cast. He'd have to do something about it. But what? That was what he had to figure out. For now he'd keep his mouth shut and act as if he accepted her decision. He mumbled, "If that's the way it's going to be, I'll just have to go along."

"Yes, you will. I'm sorry if it upsets you, but that's my decision."

Jim couldn't believe the courage of the little Dutch housewife. He knew Sylvia's presence endangered them all, but it was the only thing to do. But he was still suspicious of what Jacob might do. He wouldn't put much past him. Realistically though, there wasn't much he could do. If he tipped off the Nazis, he too would be implicated and probably killed.

Nels was satisfied with the outcome of the argument. He knew he could trust Gretel and Jim, and he didn't think Jacob had any option but to go along. After warming himself by the fire and drinking a mug of weak tea, he took his leave, satisfied that all was well there—at least for the time being.

Almost every week Gretel, Jim and Jacob listened to the B.B.C. broadcasts out of London. In February they heard of the Roosevelt, Churchill and Stalin meetings at Yalta. It appeared the end of the war in Europe was fast approaching, and the big three were planning for the occupation after it ended. In the middle of February they learned that Dresden had been destroyed by a firestorm after Allied bombing raids. Gretel was horrified by all the civilians killed in the fire, but Jim argued it was necessary to undermine the morale of the German people and hasten their surrender.

Fortunately, for reasons known only to the Nazis, there were few house searches during that part of the winter, and it was only necessary to get Sylvia down in the hole beneath the house a few times. But the food shortages were worse than ever. They all suffered grievously from malnutrition.

Talking to Sylvia was like a liberal education for Jim. One day she confided her anxieties, "I don't think I've discussed how they persecuted us after the Germans took over."

"You did tell me a few things, but not too much."

"First off, we were all forced to wear large red badges identifying us as Jewish—the Star of David."

"What was that all about? You were all citizens of the city like everybody else."

"We weren't after they took over. Rumors were rampant. I was scared to death. I thought we'd all be shot. They had this nasty man in charge of our neighborhood. He kept telling us we'd all be relocated to another location. We could take our personal belongings, we'd be treated well, and everything would be all right. Nobody was convinced, but we wanted to believe so much, I think we almost convinced ourselves. Papa buried all our jewelry and silver in the basement when we heard they were going to confiscate it. Then things settled down. It seemed like our fears were exaggerated."

"Really?"

"But it was only the calm before the storm. One bitter cold morning we were all called out on the street. That evil Nazi had several troopers with him who were armed to the teeth. It was so cold everybody was shaking. Papa had told me they'd never take the children. The Nazi read off a long list of the men and Papa was on the list. They were all told they were to be ready with their personal effects the next day for deportation, but that it would be all right. They'd be taken to work camps in Poland where they'd be safe. Papa reassured us it would work out, not to worry."

"Did it work out?"

"The next morning mother and I and my brother watched from the window. The men were all loaded into army trucks and taken away. Mother was beside herself. She couldn't stop crying. We all wanted to believe the Nazi, but nobody really trusted him."

"Did you hear what happened to your father?"

Sylvia choked up, "No, never, never for sure."

"I'm so sorry."

After she regained composure she said, "But these stories kept circulating through the ghetto. We heard they had been taken to a concentration camp where the able bodied were forced to work on German munitions."

"So, the stories were at least partly true."

"I guess, but the rumors got worse and worse. That they were going to take all of us, women and children and the aged. My old uncle had been spared the first deportation since he was too weak to work. He lived with us."

"What happened to him?"

"Uncle Gordon decided I'd have to be hidden in the basement. At least they'd make a place for me down there so if everybody was called I'd be safe."

"Did that reassure you?"

"A little, perhaps. But I didn't want to be separated from my mother and brother."

"What happened then?"

"After a few weeks everybody was called out. Uncle Gordon had built this hideout in the basement for me stocked with food and water, and he bundled me down there. It didn't matter what I thought. He was my elder. Mother and the rest of the family were taken away in trucks."

"Oh my God, Sylvia! What a story. It's almost beyond belief. How could man be so inhumane? I'll never understand it. You know, in America we were never told what was going on in Germany, let alone in Holland."

"I found out later they were taken to concentration camps. I don't know whether they're dead or alive." With this Sylvia dissolved in tears.

Jim gave her a big hug. She cried on his shoulder. The battle-hardened pilot was shaken to the core. He had experienced an epiphany. How it was possible for what he had considered harmless racial bias, to morph into unspeakable violence toward an entire race? That was what had happened in Germany under the evil leadership of Hitler. He collected his thoughts and tried to reassure her, "The war is almost over, Sylvia. It's very possible they'll be rescued by the advancing Russians."

"I can't talk any more tonight, Jim. But I do appreciate your encouragement, even though I doubt they're still alive."

"Keep your hopes up, I'll see you tomorrow."

In subsequent visits Jim tried several times to get her to tell some more about her family, but she seemed unwilling or unable to handle it. He regaled her with stories about life in America and this seemed to cheer her up. She was fascinated by American history. She was heartened for a time when he told her perhaps she could immigrate to the United States after the war and get away from all the dreadful hatred in Europe.

One evening after they had all eaten their dinner together in the kitchen, she was feeling better. Gretel and Jacob had gone to bed early. She brought up the subject again. "I guess, my friend, I never told you the rest of my story in Rotterdam."

"I wondered about that. What was it like down there in the basement?"

"It was awful, but I was safe. Not like my family. There was this lady, our landlady actually, who risked her life to help me. She'd come down and talk to me every evening when it was safe. She brought me food and water, after mine ran out. She was so good to me, an older woman, sort of motherly."

"She wasn't Jewish?"

"Not at all. I think she was Christian, or maybe even agnostic. She never actually said."

"Was there any word about your family?"

"Not a word." Sylvia fought back her tears.

"How'd you get out of there?"

"Somehow she knew a friend who was in the underground. She got word to him. They came to get me in the middle of the night. That was when I met Nels."

"Where did they take you?"

"He and another man had a car. They took me out of Rotterdam. I hid in the trunk. They had fake papers. When the Nazis stopped us, they got away with it. They were good talkers. I guess the Germans were dumb enough to believe their story. Nels told me later they were ready to shoot their way through the checkpoint."

"What a story. I'd like to write this up some day."

"It's not just a story. It really happened."

"I'm sorry I said that. I know it did." He gave her a hug.

"How'd you get all the way to Groot?"

"I lived with this group of resistance fighters for several weeks in the woods. It was real exciting. We moved around a lot to keep away from the Germans. It was difficult sleeping on the ground with a bunch of men. But they were good to me. Nobody did anything to me. I'm sure Nels wouldn't have stood for it."

"It's a long way to Groot from Rotterdam."

"It sure is. Nels thought Gretel would be willing to take me in. One dark night we made the trip here. It was scary. We were stopped several times, but again he had I.D. papers and we got away with it. He'd put me in the trunk when we approached the checkpoints. He seemed to know right where they were. I'm so lucky to be here, but I'm afraid for all of you."

"Don't worry. The news is good. It looks like the end of the war is near."

Despite the news, food was scarcer than ever. Gretel spent many hours in town every day trying to find something to buy. One afternoon, after a discouraging day with little result, she returned with frightening news. She had been told by a friend, who seemed to always know what was going on, that an American lieutenant had been captured by the Nazis. At first she was unconcerned. These things happened periodically. It might or might not be true. But when she heard a description of this man, she wondered, if just possibly, it could be Jim's missing copilot.

That evening after their meal, when Jacob and Sylvia were in their rooms, she brought the subject up. "Jim, I hate to tell you this. But today I heard that a young American lieutenant had been apprehended by the Gestapo. They found him hiding in a little hovel out in the woods near Metternich. I remember you told me your copilot bailed out and must be hiding somewhere, and that Nels didn't know anything about his whereabouts."

"Did you get any information about what he looked like?"

"It was fragmentary at best."

Jim looked apprehensive, "Tell me what you heard."

"They said he was tall, dark haired and good looking."

"Oh, my God, that might be Bill Richter, my copilot."

"Was he in uniform?"

"The word is he was not."

"He'll be treated like a spy."

"You're probably right."

"The only hope is the war will end before they do away with him. Bill was a nice guy, from a little town in Indiana. I never thought he was ready for those bombing missions. He was too nervous. But he didn't deserve this, if it really is him."

"I'm sorry to bring you such bad news, but I knew you'd expect to be told."

"I'm glad you did. I'll tell Nels, maybe they can rescue him. We don't really know for sure if it's him."

"That's right. Would you like another cup of tea?"

"I would." Jim sank into deep thought. One of his greatest fears all along had been that the Germans would get the rest of his crew. But as time passed he was too busy with Sylvia to give it much thought. The lack of any news was in a way encouraging, since the Germans loved to publicize their successes and he hadn't heard a thing.

When Nels showed up on his next visit, Jim asked, "Do you have any information on who they captured?"

"I'm sorry to tell you this, but we're sure it's your copilot. He matches the description you gave perfectly. His story is stranger than fiction. He was picked up by an elderly farmer. Apparently, he'd been injured when he hit the ground. He had a damaged ankle and it became infected. This farmer got him into town to a doctor he knew about. He treated him with penicillin and he got better. We gather he was in hiding for quite a time before the Nazis caught up with him. It sounds like the doctor protected him. Where he was hidden we don't know. Later on the Germans were tipped off and caught up with him. He was in bad shape hiding in a hunter's shed, in deep woods. Who tipped them off we don't know for sure, but we suspect the doctor. Why he would do this we haven't been able to figure out, after all he'd done for him. The doctor was known as an ardent enemy of the occupation. No one thought of this good man as a collaborator. But you never know about people in these troubled times."

Jim grimaced, "That's the worst news I've had yet. Poor Bill. I liked him a lot. If you hear anything more about how this came about, would you let me know? Someday I'll have to tell his family, if they do kill him. I strongly suspect they will, those bastards."

"Listen, Jim, the resistance will do everything it can to rescue him. But don't get your hopes up. It's virtually impossible. We're not even sure where he's been taken, and they'll have him heavily guarded."

"I understand, but please try. All I can think about is his family back home. He was their only son."

"You can be sure of that. I've got to get back to my colleagues. Things are heating up. We're spending most of our time just trying not to get caught. I'll see you later." Nels disappeared out the back door, not even staying to talk to Gretel.

After the sad news, Jim went into a funk. Now all he could think about was the fate of the rest of the crew. He dragged through his daily routines and avoided telling Gretel or Sylvia what had happened. Things were bad enough with the shortage of food and the threat of another search and he didn't want to add to their worries.

Gretel came back one day from the village with the news, "I hate to tell you all this. But the word is out that the Nazis are bringing another police dog to help in the searches."

They sat in stunned silence. Jacob's face darkened, "Now, it's come to this. We've got to get Sylvia out of here. They're sure to find her now with that dog. You know what happened the last time. We were only saved by Fang. It's a desperate situation. We've got to act."

Sylvia had overheard this remark and was panic stricken.

Jim shouted, "Will you shut up! We aren't going to turn her over, and that's that! We'll just have to figure out a new plan."

Gretel said, "Listen, Jacob, I told you before. I'm going to protect her with my life. If you can't go along, you can get out."

Jacob reddened, "If you can't do it, then I will. It's either her or us." He jumped up and rushed back to their bedroom, not willing to face her anger. Now he'd done it. He'd told them what he'd been thinking all along. The time for thinking was past. He'd have to figure out how to turn her over, and do it right away. It had to be done so the Germans couldn't figure out she'd been hiding there.

Jim agonized over what to do. He knew Jacob had to be dealt with. Time was running out. It was apparent that he was intent on outing Sylvia, which meant sure death for the poor girl. He thought seriously of shooting him, but he'd have to talk it over with Nels first. Between the two of them they could figure it out. Nels knew more about dealing with collaborators like Jacob than he did. He'd always thought Jacob was just talking, but it had gone beyond mere talk. During the next weeks Jim anxiously watched Jacob for fear that he might act before Nels came back. He had no way of getting word to Nels. He'd just have to wait until he showed up.

CHAPTER XVIII

"He's always been a big talker."

April, 1945, Groot, Holland

As spring approached in the little safe house, with the good news from the war fronts, Jim's fears abated. Jacob showed no inclination of carrying out his evil threat. Perhaps it was only idle talk after all, but Jim watched his every move just to be sure. Gretel had agreed to accompany him whenever he went out. Sylvia was encouraged by the Allied advances, and hoped against hope that the Russians might rescue her family.

One morning before Jacob got up Gretel was in the kitchen busily preparing their meager breakfast. "You know, Jim, I never did believe that Jake would do such a horrid thing. He's always been a big talker."

"I hope you're right."

"I'm going into town today. See if I can get some food. We're almost out. Nels hasn't brought us anything for quite a while. Maybe if I go real early I'll have a chance."

"Is there anything I can do to help?"

"You're doing a lot already, taking care of Sylvia. How's she feeling?"

"A little better. Gained some weight. Still not too strong."

"I'll be off now. Tell Jake I had to go out."

"Sure thing." Jim thought it'd be hard to tell him anything. They hadn't spoken in weeks since the last run-in.

Gretel hurried out with her shopping basket, always hopeful she'd have better luck this time. It was a bright sunny morning with a promise of spring. It felt good to be warmed by the sun. When she arrived at the village square she was surprised to see a crowd of people in front of the city hall. With the occupation, the citizens were seldom out on the street.

Spotting a friend of hers, she asked, "Emma, what's going on here?"

"Oh, Gretel, how are you? I haven't seen you in a long time."

"I'm all right. What's going on?"

"There's bad news. The Gestapo claims they've captured an American spy."

"I already heard that."

"But there's more. Just look at this."

She handed over a copy of the Amsterdam paper. Gretel nervously studied the front page. She couldn't believe her eyes. There was a dreadful picture. The victim at the end of the noose looked exactly like Jim's description of his copilot. "Could I borrow this? It looks like an American I heard about."

Her friend looked puzzled, "How would you know about an American?"

Gretel realized she had said too much. "I was only talking. You know, you hear all of these stories. Probably just gossip. Could you lend it to me?"

"I will, but bring it back. My husband loves to read the paper. Even with all the German propaganda. He doesn't have much else to do."

"Thank you so much, Emma. I'll be sure to bring it back."

She forgot her shopping and hurried right home with the paper and the grisly news. Entering the house she found Jim and Jacob sitting gloomily by the little fire in the kitchen.

"Jim, take a look at this." She handed him the front page.

He studied the picture of the hanging carefully. His expression said it all.

"Oh, my God! It's Bill! I'm sure of it. It's my copilot, Bill. Those bastards hung him."

"I was afraid you'd say that. I'm so sorry."

"It's barbaric. How could they do such a thing? He should have been a prisoner of war. What about the international laws of warfare?"

"I don't know about that. Was he your friend?"

"Not exactly. My regular copilot got shot up. Was in the hospital. Bill had just been assigned to my ship. He was only a kid. A nice young guy from Indiana. Sort of green, but he was learning. Those rotten sons-of-bitches!"

Jim looked distraught. He slumped in the chair. "Could you read it to me?"

Gretel read the grim words.

American Spy Captured by the Gestapo

> *A patriotic Dutch doctor has turned over an American airman to the authorities. Dressed in civilian clothes, he was caught stealing military secrets. Investigations are underway to determine who might have aided him. The guilty parties will be apprehended and executed.*
>
> *All patriotic Dutchmen are proud of the valiant efforts of the Gestapo in dealing with this threat to the nation's security. Let this be a lesson to those who may be protecting the enemy.*

Gretel struggled to explain, "They're trying to terrify the people. They know other Allied airmen are being protected by Dutch patriots. It's getting worse since they're losing the war. I heard that Hitler might order all prisoners of war executed."

In the ensuing days Jim was depressed, so unlike his usual self, when he seemed able to handle the pressures of hiding out so well. He was saddened at the fate of Bill and even more apprehensive for the rest of the crew. It was strange he hadn't heard a word from the underground about them. He tried hard to put a good face on it in his visits with Sylvia, but she was perceptive and quickly discerned that he was unhappy.

CHAPTER XIX

"This was just further evidence of the duplicity of the Americans."

April-May, 1945: Groot, Holland

In *April of1945 Germany's situation was becoming desperate. Russia's armies were massed in overpowering force, poised to take Berlin. Hitler had moved his headquarters to a bunker deep below the Chancellery. On the 12th of April Roosevelt died at Warm Springs, Georgia, tragically unable to see the end of the war he had been so instrumental in winning. Despite the deteriorating situation, Hitler continued to pursue his reign of terror throughout Europe. In Holland, on Hitler's birthday, they hanged a Dutchman, Anton Holzel, from the town of Deventer. Rumors were rampant that Hitler would order the execution of all POW's. The Dutch feared widespread reprisals throughout the country.*

Jacob was preoccupied with fears about the Jewish girl. The hanging of the copilot had proved, without a doubt, what would happen to them if they did find her. He'd be killed despite his sympathy for the German cause. He had to figure out how to turn her over without implicating himself.

One morning after a restless night it came to him. He would abduct her in the night, take her out to the nearby woods, leave her to fend for herself, and probable capture. The Germans would never know where she had been hidden, and she would never tell. When Gretel and Jim realized she was missing, there would be no reason to suspect him. Even if they did, there wouldn't be any proof. He had to carefully plan every detail to make his scheme foolproof. How could he avoid rousing Gretel when he left the bedroom? How could he bind and gag Sylvia before she called out? This required careful planning, something he'd been good at in business.

On a pleasantly warm spring night Nels arrived at the back door. The residents were huddled around the iron stove to fend off the chill of the dank building. The warmth outside hadn't yet penetrated the stone of the old house.

After the customary greetings Jim told his friend the story, "Nels, did you hear that Bill Richter, my copilot, was executed by the Gestapo? Hanged in a public square."

"I did."

"What bothers me most is why this doctor, who was known to be hostile to the Germans, would do such a thing."

"I have some information on that."

Jim flushed, raising his voice, "What is it, man? Tell me!"

Gretel and Jacob listened, determined not to miss a word.

Nels hated to go on, but he'd already admitted he knew about the hanging. He had no choice but to reveal the unpleasant news, "I dislike telling you this, but I know you'll find out some day and blame me for not telling you."

"Please go on."

"Well, it seems Doctor DeVries, an older doctor, had taken a beautiful young wife from a poor family in Metternich. It was the talk of the town. Anyway, Lieutenant Richter was brought there by a friendly farmer. He injured his ankle when he hit the ground. The doctor treated the infection with penicillin and cured it. He worked out an arrangement with a friend of his, a local dominei, and secreted him in the parsonage. The doctor's young wife cared for him. It seems that your colleague seduced her. When Doctor DeVries found out, he was furious. He turned the Lieutenant over to the Nazis as reprisal.

Jim reddened, "I can't believe it. Bill wouldn't do a thing like that. He was a decent young guy from a small town in Indiana. How do you know that?"

"Well, my friend. Suit yourself. We have a representative in the town. Sometimes war brings out the best and the worst in people."

"What an evil thing. Bill did that to the man that saved his life?"

"Apparently, he did. You must realize the power of sexual attraction in a young man. He was away from home with no sexual outlet. He was attracted by a pretty young thing, who was probably bored with her life with the old gentleman. I think he swept her off her feet with his attentions. I'm not justifying what he did, just trying to understand it."

"Don't tell me about sexual attraction. I'm young too. He must have been well fed. If you're hungry enough you lose all interest. Listen, Nels, I'm sorry I lost my temper. I should of known better."

Gretel was disturbed by the tension in the room. She broke in, "Gentlemen, how about a nice cup of tea? I've even got some biscuits left over."

They relaxed as they sipped their tea. For the moment, at least, Jim forgot about the sordid story of his copilot.

Jacob was bored listening to their conversation. He stood up and turned to Gretel, "Dear, it's a pleasant night. I'll go outside and collect some firewood."

"All right, Jake. We're getting low. Watch out for the patrols."

After he left, Nels asked, "Jim, has Jacob made any more threats about the girl?"

"He's been strangely quiet. Haven't heard a word. Don't know what's going on."

Gretel looked upset, "Don't worry about him. He'd never do anything to her. He was only talking. Why would he, anyway? He hopes to get his business back."

Jim said, "You never know. There's an old saying in the states, where there's smoke there's fire."

Nels leaned forward, looking her right in the eyes, "Gretel, I don't want to upset you. Have you seen anything unusual he's done lately?"

There was a pregnant silence in the room as she puzzled over the question. The fire crackled. The flames flared up for an instant, momentarily brightening the gloomy kitchen. They waited eagerly to hear what she might say.

Gretel wrestled with her conscience, torn by conflicting impulses—her love for Jacob and her need to be honest with her friends.

At long last she spoke hesitantly, "There was one little thing that seemed odd. I'm sure it doesn't mean a thing."

Nels searched her face. She avoided his eyes. "What is it?" He asked. "What is this little thing?"

She whispered apprehensively, "Well, I found a coil of rope under our bed."

"Rope?" He jumped up, "Why didn't you tell us before?"

She was appalled at his reaction, "I just saw it. It probably doesn't mean a thing. Maybe he wanted to tie the wood together."

"Why would it be under the bed?"

"I don't know. Men do some strange things sometimes."

"Could it have been there before?"

"Absolutely not. I clean under there every week. It didn't mean a thing to me. What would he want rope for?"

"It's hard to say. I'm sure it doesn't amount to anything. Gretel, could you let Jim and me talk privately for a while? There are some things we need to discuss."

"I'd be glad to. I've been tired lately. Think I'll go to bed early."

"Get some rest. I'll let myself out. Good night."

Jim added, "Good night, Gretel. See you in the morning."

She hurried back to her bedroom, pleased to get away from his questions.

It was clear to both men that they had to act. But who was to carry out the killing? Neither one wanted to do it. But they had no choice. It had to be done.

Jim stared into the fire, watching as it crackled and hissed, puzzling over what to say. Suddenly, he yelled, "I'll do it. I hate that son-of-a-bitch. He's mine. I've never liked the thought of killing anybody in cold blood. But I'd relish this one."

"Wait just a minute. I'm the underground fighter. I'm in charge. I'll take care of him. I have more experience with this type of thing than you."

"I suppose you do. But you haven't lived with him all these months. You haven't seen how rotten he is. I knew he was a collaborator long before you did."

"I hate to bring this up Jim. What about your attitude toward the Jews? I thought you had some anti-Semitic attitudes. You're willing to kill this man because he's planning to out a Jewish girl?"

"That's a thing of the past. I'll never feel like that again. I've learned knowing Sylvia how wrong I was. This thing that has happened throughout Europe is the most monstrous act in the history of mankind. This genocide has got to stop. I had no idea what was going on until I got over here. What happened to Bill proves we've gotta act. Right away."

"At least we agree on that. I've got an idea. I know that deep down neither one of us wants to look him in the eye and shoot him."

"You're right about that. What's your idea?"

"Let's draw straws. The winner does the deed. That's fair, isn't it?"

Jim sat quietly mulling over the fateful choice. He had killed many people but on bombing runs at altitude. The idea of shooting a defenseless man like that appalled him, but he wasn't admitting it. On the other hand he had more personal hatred than Nels. He'd been around him week after week and month after month, seen his duplicity with kind Gretel, and his hatred of Sylvia. For Nels he thought it would be just another assignment, mission accomplished.

The flames shot up brightening the dreary room. The wet wood hissed and crackled. They alternately stared into the fire or glanced at each other, trying to read the other guy's thoughts. The minutes dragged on as the cuckoo clock on the shelf tick tocked.

Nels exploded, "Well, what's it gonna be? You or me? Let's draw straws. That'll be fair."

"You're on! I'll do it. Draw the fucking straws. This's it. Get on with it man, before I change my mind. I still think he should be mine but I'll go along to satisfy you."

"Good!" Nels almost shouted. "Let's get it over with." He went over into the corner and extracted two straws from Gretel's broom, one long and one short. "I'll hold these behind my back and mix them up. You call it. I'll bring one out. If you're right he's yours. If not he's mine."

"That sounds fair. Let's do it."

Nels shuffled the straws behind his back. "What's your call?"

"I'll take the long."

When Nels brought one straw out it was the long. He studied his friend's face for a reaction. He saw a narrowing of the eyes, a contraction of the lips, a look of steely resolve. He knew this was it. Jim would carry out his deadly mission.

The flames flickered, the wood smoldered and the room darkened. It smelled of damp wood. Silence descended. Jim was pleased in a way but appalled at what he was in for. He was committed. He'd have to figure out when and how.

Nels got up, "Well, my friend. I'll be going. If you need any ideas how to do it, I've got some."

Jim gritted his teeth, "Don't worry about me. Good night. They shook hands to bind the deal.

Nels left out the back door, confident they had chosen the right path. He had every confidence in his friend but you never knew about an act of this kind. It often wasn't that hard on the spur of the moment, but a calculated killing like this was difficult at best, especially to an American.

As the days passed Jim wrestled with the question of how and where he would do it. It had to be out of Gretel's sight. It had to be done without her knowledge. With his religious background he never did believe in killing, but the war had changed all that. Now, with his friendship and concern for the little girl his resolve overcame all reservations. Before going to bed that night he got out his Colt 45 and cleaned and polished it. He had decided the best opportunity would be some night when Jacob went out to collect fire wood. He'd follow him out. If he did it right, the Nazis would never know who did it.

Jim watched day by day as the supply of wood diminished. One night in May, Jacob announced, "Gretel, I've got to go out tonight and collect firewood. We're almost out."

"All right, but be careful. The Germans are tightening up again." Gretel said.

"I know the country around here better than they do. Don't worry about me."

He went back to their bedroom and put on a dark sweater and a pair of pants, pocketed his flashlight, and went out the back door with a burlap bag.

Jim quickly stood up, "I'm off to bed." He stretched. "Really tired tonight."

She said, "It's early for you. Good night, Jim."

He hurried down the hall, found his pistol in the chest and climbed out the back window, just in time to see Jacob going over the wall in back of the garden. Jim hurried to catch up, staying just far enough back to escape detection. Jacob moved slowly out of town and into a nearby wood where he started to collect dead twigs and branches. As Jim's eyes adjusted to the light, it would be an easy shot. He raised the pistol, squared Jacob's head in the sights, steadying his right hand with his left, just ready to squeeze off the shot. As sweat dripped from his brow, a thought came to him. He wanted Jacob to suffer, to realize what was happening, to anticipate his death in agonizing moments before the end.

Jacob bent over to pick up a large branch. Jim stealthily snuck up behind him and jammed the cold steel of the barrel into the back of his head.

"Now, I've got you, you dirty bastard. Put your hands up."

"What's the matter with you? Put that thing down."

With his free hand Jim shone his flashlight in Jacob's face. "Now tell me what you're planning to do to Sylvia."

"Nothing at all. Nothing. Where'd you get that idea?"

"Where'd I get it? Under the bed. That coil of rope you put there."

"What rope? Never heard of it. What are you talking about? Put that gun down."

"Prepare to meet your maker. You're the one that's gonna die now." He cocked the gun.

Jacob started to shake. He pleaded plaintively, "Please, Jim. You're wrong about me. I'd never do anything to her. That was only talk. Everybody knows I talk too much."

"You bastard, get on your knees and grovel. You're done for."

Jacob knelt down and started to sob. Jim was unmoved, enjoying every minute of it, his reservations about killing in cold blood put behind him. He was just ready to pull the trigger when the silence of the night was interrupted by the pealing of a church bell, coming from the village square. He stopped to listen, then he heard shouting and small arms fire. He could barely make out the words.

"PEACE AT LAST! GERMANY SURRENDERS!"

He turned to the groveling collaborator, "Get your sorry ass out of here! If I ever see you again I'll shoot you on sight."

Jacob took off running for his life, never to be seen again.

Jim was ecstatic. He threw his gun deep into the brush.

He'd been delivered from the dreadful responsibility of killing in cold blood. The war in Europe was over at last.

He took off at top speed in the direction of Gretel's house. As he ran he listened to the church bells, the most beautiful sound he had ever heard.

It was May 7th, 1945. Germany had surrendered unconditionally.

EPILOGUE

Captain James Scott was transported by jeep a few days later to Amsterdam where he was flown back to the states by military transport. After discharge he returned to Harvard and his graduate studies in history. Following graduation, he married Suzanne Olson, his childhood sweetheart from his home town, and became a well known historian concentrating on World War II.

Gretel Ruyschel resumed her household duties and lived happily into old age never to miss her erstwhile lover, Jacob. She corresponded regularly with Sylvia, and years later they had a reunion in Rotterdam and relived their wartime experiences together. They remained good friends for the rest of their lives.

Jacob Schimmel never recovered his business which the Nazis had destroyed. His partner, who had put up the money for their business, refused to associate with him again. Jacob worked for the rest of his life as a clerk in a small export-import business and died at a young age, a broken man.

Doctor De Vries' medical practice was destroyed when the story of his collaboration with the enemy became common knowledge in Metternich. He moved to a larger city in the south of Holland and found employment in his profession as a resident physician in a public hospital.

Johanna wrote frequently to her former husband begging forgiveness. Some years later he forgave her youthful indiscretion. He had always loved her, despite the affair with Bill Richter. They remarried, lived happily as man and wife, and raised a family of two boys and a girl.

Nels Maas rejoined his family and later resumed his studies at university. After graduation he had a successful career at the bar and became one of the political leaders of Holland.

Tragically, the rest of the crew of the ill fated B-24 all drowned in the Zuider Zee. American intelligence ascertained that they had jumped too soon and rescue attempts had failed to reach them in time. They had been unable to extricate themselves from their chutes to avoid drowning. A government inquiry exonerated Captain Scott determining that they had bailed out before he had given the command to jump.

Sylvia Zimmerman's mother, brother and uncle were executed in the gas chambers, but her father had managed to survive working in a munitions plant. In ill health for the rest of his life, Sylvia took care of her father until he died. She then married a Jewish man about her age and had a family of three children. For the rest of her life she suffered from nightmares reliving the horrors of the Holocaust.

REFERENCES

Ambrose, Stephen; No End Save Victory, Vol. I; www.Amazon.com.

Cross, Rubin; The Battle of the Bulge, BBC, Internet.

Gilbert, Martin; the Second World War, G.P. Putnam &Co., New York City, 1970.

Gabay, John; Diary of a Tail Gunner, Internet, Google.

The Netherlands in Cold War II, Wikopedia, the Free Encyclopedia, from Google, Internet.

Polsson, Ken; Chronology of World War II, Google, Internet, 2998.

Wiese, Elie; Night, Bantam Books, Random House, Inc. NYC, 1960.

Woolf, Linda; Survival and Resistance, the Netherlands Uunder Nazi Occupation, Google, Internet.

The Mighty Eighth: A museum dedicated to the Eighth Air Force outside Savannah, Georgia.

THE END

Edwards Brothers, Inc.
Thorofare, NJ USA
May 14, 2011